Just Joe

by
William Siems

Just Joe

Publised Summer 2024 by William Siems

ISBN: 9798990041349

First printing - Summer 2024

Scripture quotations from the SUV (Siems Unauthorized Version) of the Bible

Contact the author at chayeem10@gmail.com

Cover by Jacob Bridgman

Interior design by Alane Pearce of Professional Writing Services LLC contact at MyPublishingCoach.com/contact

Dedication

In 2017, I published the first of my two apocalyptic novels followed by five Biblical adventures. In early 2024, I departed from those to write a semi-autobiographical contemporary Christian novel, *"School Daze,"* only to find that it was linked back to the first two. This current volume, *"Just Joe,"* is set in the same time frame as my eighth. As always, I was surprised by who showed up and what unexpectedly happened.

Again, without the faithful support of many this would have remained the whimsical musings of a guy lost in his fanciful thinking. Thanks to the constant encouragement of my wife, the faithful few readers who kept asking, "What's next?" and my compassionately brutal editor, who makes sense of my scribbling. Thanks to my dog, Stacy, whom the neighbors took care of for me. Part of my reprieves from writing was my daily visit to her, but she has gone on to a "better place." Most of all, thanks to the One who continues to give me dreams and visions of books to come, Jesus the Messiah. Blessings…

Summer 2024
William Siems

Dedication

Table of Contents

Chapter One - The Beginning 7
Chapter Two - Sixth and Eisenhower 11
Chapter Three - Dining Hall 15
Chapter Four - Second Year at John Wesley 17
Chapter Five - Another Occupation 19
Chapter Six - The Bully 23
Chapter Seven - Rabbi Levi Shammah 27
Chapter Eight - The Rabbi Speaks 33
Chapter Nine - Nurse and Systems Analyst 37
Chapter Ten - Meeting HR and IT 41
Chapter Eleven - Thursday at Dragoon 45
Chapter Twelve - Another Late Dinner 49
Chapter Thirteen - Elise 51
Chapter Fourteen - Monday with the IUSR 55
Chapter Fifteen - Accents 59
Chapter Sixteen - Job Complete? 61
Chapter Seventeen - Monday's Assignment 67
Chapter Eighteen - The Tim-DOS Award 71
Chapter Nineteen - Work, Work, Work 75
Chapter Twenty - An Earlier Lunch 77
Chapter Twenty-One - Garage-ware 81
Chapter Twenty-Two - Elise's Home 85
Chapter Twenty-Three - Not Just Another Day 87
Chapter Twenty-Four - Sabbath's End 93
Chapter Twenty-Five - After the Conference 97
Chapter Twenty-Six - A New Chapter 101
Chapter Twenty-Seven - A New Day 105
Chapter Twenty-Eight - Beginning That Friday 109
Chapter Twenty-Nine - Another Sabbath Service 113
Chapter Thirty - The Recovery Specialist 115
Chapter Thirty-One - Back at Chick-fil-A 119
Chapter Thirty-Two - Trip to the Farm 123
Chapter Thirty-Three - Preparations 129

Chapter Thirty-Four - The Farm Again 133
Chapter Thirty-Five - More Synchronicity 137
Chapter Thirty-Six - The Children's Home 141
Chapter Thirty-Seven - Sheep & Elaine 145
Chapter Thirty-Eight - First Surprise 149
About the Author 153

Chapter One
The Beginning

Joe Huddleston met Elaine Swanson in college, in a first year philosophy class they shared. Joe had seated himself early, as usual, and had his head buried in the class syllabus, checking out the required texts and the dates of the exams and when the class' papers would be due. Suddenly, he was enveloped in the most wonderful aroma. There was a hint of rose, vanilla, and maybe apple, all expertly woven together. She sat down next to him, smiled, and he nearly melted.

She reached out a hand, "Elaine."

He wanted to bring it to his lips and kiss it, but he restrained himself to lightly taking her fingertips in his hand and responding, with "Joe."

She had dimples and her eyes actually sparkled. "Is that short for Joseph?"

He reluctantly let go of her fingers and looked down, "Nope, short for Joe," and he too grinned slightly.

Elaine continued, "So, when you were in trouble did your mother use your middle name?" And her light laughter tinkled.

"Nope, she just called out, 'JD you get in here, right now!'"

"Ah, so what does the 'D' stand for?" Laughter still echoed in her voice.

"Nothing, the 'D' is just the initial 'D,' but she couldn't call out 'Joe D' 'cause that would sound like a girl's name." It made perfect sense and they shared a laugh.

The professor was legendary, and affectionately called "Thinkernoodle" or just "Noodle" for short. Professor Noodle interrupted everyone's general conversation and settling in by saying, "Get in groups of two or three and answer the question, 'What makes man superior to the animals?', jotting down your answers. You have fifteen minutes."

Joe made a hand motion between the two of them asking if they should become a twosome. She nodded. They turned towards each other as Joe said, "Are we even sure that man is superior to the animals?"

Elaine chuckled, "I think for the purposes of our time together on this question, right now, yes."

Joe continued, "Okay then, humor. Man has a sense of humor."

Elaine smiled, "Do you have any animals?"

Joe frowned, "No, but I visit my neighbor's dog a lot and while she's excited to see me, I have never gotten the feeling that she is laughing at me."

Elaine looked him straight in the eye, "I'm pretty sure that every time my cat comes to me in the kitchen, she is saying to herself, '*Watch how I will get her to feed me even though it isn't even close to meal time,*' and laughs. It sounds like a meow, but subtly different."

Joe looked at the floor between them, "Hmmm, you may have a point there."

Elaine continued, "I'm also pretty sure that my cat thinks she's either a person herself or at least equal to a person."

"Hmmm, another point, but what makes us different if not humor?"

"My cat gets stressed out any time I start cleaning for a party or packing a suitcase. But worry? I have never seen anything resembling worry from my cat." Elaine was racking up points left and right.

"Hmmm, what about planning? Do you think animals plan?" Joe asked.

Elaine thought a minute and then responded, "Probably in the wild. The predator would plan his next attack and the prey might plan how to escape the next attack rather than just relying on luck."

It was Joe's turn. "Animals seem to be happy, sad, and show love. Having emotions would seem to indicate that they have souls."

"I hadn't thought of it like that, but, yeah, it would. What about spirits, do they have spirits?" she said thoughtfully.

"Good question," Joe smiled. She nodded. "The third chapter in Ecclesiastes says," and he looked it up:

"For what happens to the children of man and what happens to the beasts is the same; as one dies, so dies the other. They all have the same breath, and man has no advantage over the beasts, for all is vanity. All go to one place. All are from the dust, and to dust all return. Who knows whether the spirit of man goes upward and the spirit of the beast goes down into the earth?"

"They all have the same breath. The word for breath, in the Hebrew, is the same word for spirit." And he went on, "Dust is dust, that's the body, but the spirit endures and goes somewhere, up or down who knows, but somewhere."

Elaine smiled, "Humans have a larger brain that man doesn't use very well."

Joe smiled in return, "Does that go just for men or for women too?"

She reached over and punched him lightly on the shoulder, "Both, silly."

"And an ability to walk erect on only two legs," he added.

"Monkeys do that, and also have an opposable thumb for grasping." She paused, "We're not doing very well."

"Poetry, what about poetry?" Joe asked confidently.

She snickered, "I suppose you speak monkey and can verify that they don't compose poetry."

Joe perked up, "Actually I do, and it's an international language. I went to our zoo and just for fun, outside the primate house, began speaking to a single monkey sitting on a limb in the outside cage all by himself. He got very excited and we chatted back and forth for a few minutes. Years later, when I was in China, I was at the Beijing zoo and thought I'd see if I could chat with a monkey there. Sure enough I could. I cannot, however, affirm that they compose poetry."

Professor Noodle called the class back to order, "Okay, what separates us from the animals?" Joe raised his hand and professor Noodle pointed at him, "Yes?"

Joe smiled, "Poetry, sir, animals do not write poetry." The class snickered and Elaine just shook her head. Other hands went up and Noodle called on them and wrote their answers on the whiteboard. During the discussion, Elaine looked down at her desk and found a note, "When are you done with classes today?"

She covered the paper, cupping her hand around it and wrote, "3pm," and passed it unobtrusively back to Joe.

He added, "Coffee or something after that?" and held it down low by his leg so she could take it without being seen.

She added, "Bistro on Sixth and Eisenhower," and held it down by her own leg.

He took it, read it, and gave her a thumbs up.

Chapter Two
Sixth and Eisenhower

Elaine entered the Metronome Bistro on Sixth and Eisenhower about ten minutes after three. She looked around slowly. Finally she spied him near the back, at a table for two, by the window. She waved. He saw her and started to get up. She gestured for him to stay there and went up to the counter to ordered her Chai-nog Latte. She paid for it and stood in line until it was ready. Then she joined Joe at the table.

He stood as she approached the table and then sat down when she did. "So, what's your poison?" he asked pointing at her cup.

She laughed quietly, "A Chai-nog Latte," and held it out proudly.

"So, how was the rest of your day?" He smiled a bit shyly.

She began, "Not as much fun as philosophy. My chemistry teacher is good, but that's not my favorite subject. Lit was good, we are going to read *'Beowulf'*, and I'm sure I will enjoy comp. I felt a little weak in my high school algebra, so college level algebra will help me fix that. How about you?" She matched his smile, but without the shyness.

He ran through his class schedule, "Music appreciation should be easy, as well as calculus." When he saw that she blanched, he added, "Sorry. My lit class is starting with a section on poetry, which matches my comp class. We have to bring in an original poem and I don't think *'Roses are red, violets are blue,'* will cut it. My science class is physics, which I am sure I will enjoy."

She wiped her brow, "Whew, a pretty full load for both of us. How will we have time for romance?" He looked up startled, until she added, "And it will take a while for you to understand my sense of humor."

He sighed and looked at the table, "Did you get your books before classes started?"

"Yes, and I appreciated that they each came with a class syllabus, so we could hit the ground running."

"It's so easy to get behind and then you are in big trouble."

She looked him straight in the eye, "So, what brought you to John Wesley U?"

He held her eyes a moment and then left her gaze, "I grew up as an Anglican, so wanted something less secular than the State university. I could have stepped up to a good Catholic university, but wanted to stay closer to my roots. So, this was my next choice. I looked at their curriculum, came and did a weekend visit, and was impressed. So, here I am. What about you?"

She smiled a little shyly, "My story is similar, but from the other direction. I was raised Baptist and was looking for something a little less rigid. Not that I regret my upbringing. It probably kept me out of trouble in high school," and she snickered

"You were in danger of getting into trouble?" Joe was smiling.

"Not wild," and she paused, "but perhaps a little rebellious. It was a Baptist high school and it seemed a little stifling. Coming here seemed like it would be a breath of fresh air. Maybe it's just a chance to be out on my own and not pressured into making the decisions that are made to please someone else."

"*Hmm,*" and he mused out loud, "I think I might have wanted to be assured of a more positive tone to any peer pressure." Now he paused before he continued, "Does that sound a little immature?"

He thought he could sense a warm compassion underlying her reply as she said, "No, that sounds more like wisdom than immaturity."

Joe smiled faintly, "Are you finding what you hoped for?"

Elaine winked, "I think so." He reached his hand across the table. She looked down at it, "A little early for hand holding, Joe."

He slowly brought it back, "Can't blame a guy for trying."

She chuckled, "I could, but I won't."

Joe tried another tack, "Dinner?"

She looked in her purse, rummaged around, pulled out a card and showed him, "Meal ticket. You didn't buy one?"

He looked away, "Naw, I figured that institutionalized food would be terrible."

"Didn't you eat here when you visited?" she countered.

"Hmmm," he thought a moment. "I did and it was pretty good. Can I join you at the dining hall?"

It was her turn to look away, "I'm meeting some gal friends."

His response was a disheartened, "Oh."

She tried to sound cheery, "But I'll see you in philosophy tomorrow and you can show me your better than 'roses are red' poem."

He did cheer up a bit at that, "Sounds like a plan." He pushed his chair back from the table and stood. "I'll see you then." He turned quickly and walked away thinking to himself, "*Take it slow Joey boy, nice and slow,*" and vowed to make his poem smashing.

Chapter Three
Dining Hall

Elaine walked towards the table they had started choosing, the one at the windows, looking out at the campus meadow that was surrounded on three sides by trees. As usual, she was right on time, Julie and Lucy were early, and Lannie would show up fashionably late. Elaine waved.

Lucy began, "You are looking at the newest reporter for the University paper."

Elaine blanched, "Oh no! Does that mean we must be on our best behavior?"

Julie chimed in, "And be careful what we say?"

Lucy was smiling from ear to ear, "No, you just have to preface everything with 'This is off the record,'" and she laughed out loud. Lannie finally straggled in and sat down.

"Whew, here we are having just begun and already I feel frantic." The others all smiled.

Elaine responded, "Lannie, has there ever been a time in recent history when you haven't felt frantic?"

Lannie thought a moment, "Hmm, point taken."

Elaine sat up a little straighter, "Well, I have met someone." They all leaned forward. "I met him in philosophy class and we met after all our classes today. He even invited me to dinner, but I had to meet with you." She showed a mock frown.

Lannie frowned back, "I think you could have called us and begged off for the night."

Elaine came right back with, "I wouldn't want to appear too easy. He actually held out his hand for me to hold while we were talking."

Julie and Lucy chimed in with, "Ahh, one of those."

"Naw," Elaine exclaimed, "he's really nice. It's just I want to take things slowly."

Lannie chimed in, "So, what are you going to do?"

Elaine sighed, "Take it slow."

Julie snickered, "If he's one of the good guys don't take it too slow. You might lose him."

Elaine frowned, "Thanks, I'll be careful. So, how are your classes?" and she looked at each of them.

The others didn't really care about the classes. They were more disappointed that none of them had met anybody like she had on the very first day.

She countered with, "Well, there's the Sorority's first dance next weekend."

They almost sighed and shrugged in concert, "That's usually attended by just a bunch of posers."

"That's what we've been told, but they haven't had us there before. Maybe this year will be different." Elaine wanted to give them some hope.

"Yeah," Lannie spoke as if the thought had just occurred to her, "maybe your friend has some friends. You've got two weeks to find them and get them to the dance. So, besides being a bit forward, tell us about this fellow."

Elaine was shaking her head as she said, "He's not forward. He was just moving a little faster than I was comfortable with. His name is Joe, he's clever, funny, and will make philosophy enjoyable. Maybe we can even pass notes," and she winked at them. They rolled their eyes.

"Seriously?" Julie asked, "Well, make sure you ask him about his friends." Elaine nodded in the affirmative.

Chapter Four
Second Year at John Wesley

Elaine felt gratified in the growth of their relationship. She had finally allowed him to hold her hand, but that was as far as the physical side of things had progressed. Not for lack of his desire. She could tell, every once in a while, he really wanted to kiss her, but he had amazing self-control. It was one of the many things that she liked and respected about him. Most everything she found out about him only increased her respect. Well, except maybe his quirky humor, like:

"An old farmer had a wife who nagged him constantly. His only solace was when he was out plowing the field. He was out peacefully plowing one day when she brought him lunch. She began to nag him about one thing or another, when suddenly his donkey reared back and kicked her in the head, killing her instantly. At the open casket funeral, a wife would come up to him, say something, and he would nod his head, 'Yes.' Afterwards her husband would come up to him, say something, and he would shake his head, 'No.' After the service, the minister approached him and asked him what was said to him. The old farmer replied, 'The wives would look into the casket and remark how good she looked in that pretty dress. Then the men would approach me and ask if the donkey was for sale."

It was a funny story, but only marginally appropriate.

They met often for lunch or after classes, but tried to keep some distance in their relationship. While they had never decided that their relationship would be exclusive, for all practical matters it was. The first quarter of their second year they had taken a literature class together, "The Great American Novel." They had read and discussed "To Kill a Mockingbird" together and even helped one another on their final papers, both which were deemed "A" papers. However, the relationship was seen as just a very deep friendship, with, now, the occasional hand holding.

The final quarter of that second year they had taken a genetics class together. It was part of her core curriculum, as she had decided to become a nurse. For him it was just for fun and would fulfill an elective requirement. Think about it, taking a genetics class for fun? They did make it fun though, through sheer force of will. Again, as they helped each other, they both received an "A" in genetics.

However, what was beginning to make things difficult was Joe's financial situation. It was becoming harder and harder to make ends meet with his meager scholarship and only working part time at a local fast food restaurant. It was probably time for a change. Joe was firmly against taking out school loans. While they seemed a good idea, because of their deferred interest, to him debt was debt, and he did not want to incur any at all. She found that another reason she respected him, his work ethic, and sound financial decision making.

Chapter Five
Another Occupation

Joe began to look for another job. He answered an ad for a small local software company and received a request for an interview. When it was his turn he walked in and sat across from a smartly dressed woman in her early thirties.

"Joe, I see you have a solid GPA. What are your plans for the future?" The interviewer seem genuinely interested, but she may have just been well trained.

"Personally, professionally, what areas are you interested in?" Joe asked tentatively.

She just smiled, "Yes."

He took a breath, "Well, to finish my degree is a given. I am not particularly into the 'house with a white picket fence' idea, but a wife and kids would be nice, and I want to work someplace where what I do will make a difference." He paused, "I'm probably out of line for saying this, but don't you have a daughter who is desperately ill."

It took a moment for the shock to register, "How could you possibly know that?"

"Well, I could be psychic or ...." He left the sentence dangling.

Her astonishment remained. "But we have never met."

"You sent me the invitation for this interview. I took a chance, looked you up, and then recognized you when I came into the room." She was still slightly shaking her head. He continued, "And..."

"And what?" she whispered.

"In my resume' you may have noticed that one of my strengths is teams?" He added.

"Yes, I did," she was practically hanging on his every word now.

He continued unabated, "I have led a couple of our second year coding projects. I shine, if that's the right word, in translating requirements into expected results. I think it's mostly because of the relationship I build with the customers. I am not too pushy and have heard that I am pleasant to work for and with. Oh, I am also humble," and he laughed self-deprecatingly as he reached into his shirt pocket and pulled out a calling card which he handed to her.

She read off the front, "Story-teller. You're a story-teller?"

His smile deepened, "And I hope that's not a euphemism for liar. It's sort of a hobby. Turn it over." She did, as he continued, "My last coding project was for the head of the university's medical department. They are doing some groundbreaking research that may apply to your daughter's illness. I mentioned your situation to him and he expects a call." Her eyes began to tear up and she found herself unable to speak. He spoke for her, "It's okay, it's just how I do what I do."

She finally found her voice, "When can you start?"

He grew a little more serious, "We should probably talk about how many hours I want to work and how much I expect to be paid." She nodded. "If I only work thirty-two hours a week, you will not have to pay me full benefits. However, I would be interested in your supplemental education package if it would still apply. I know your salaries are better than fair market value. Oh, and I have to give my fast food place two weeks notice. Does that about cover it?"

She had taken out a Kleenex and dabbed her eyes, "Was this interview just a formality?"

"No, but I think we might classify it under the category of a 'win-win' situation."

"Yes, I think so. I'll be back with a start date later this afternoon."

Joe held out his hand, "Thank you."

She was still a bit bewildered, but took his hand and looked deep into his eyes, "Thank you, too!"

Chapter Six
The Bully

Joe and Elaine had been seated in the center of Judy's Diner when a group of loud, rude and otherwise obnoxious guys entered. Their leader said something obscene and pointed towards Elaine with a, "Come with me, Babe!" Joe slowly stood, stepped around in front of the table, leaned forward, and whispered something while he made a hand gesture. Their leader looked like he had been kicked between the legs; his knees buckled and he crumpled to the floor. His cronies took two steps backwards as Joe stepped forward, leaned down, and whispered something else in the leader's ear. The man noticeably blanched and fell on his face in even more pain. Joe stood, reaching back for Elaine's hand. She took it as she rose from the table, and they walked off together.

She whispered to him, "What did you say?"

"I told him to never bother us again, or else!"

"Or else what?"

Joe smiled, "It doesn't matter, he got the message."

As the leader still cringed on his knees, one of his buddies leaned down to help him up, but got his hand swatted away while the leader struggled to his own feet. His friend asked, "What did he say to you?"

The leader had trouble standing, "He whispered something about the wind and my genitals."

His friend stepped back as though slapped, "He's a wind whisperer?"

The leader looked at him sternly, "What's that?"

"More ancient than all of the martial arts, it is said they manipulate the very fabric of the material world." Fear mixed with awe tinged his voice.

Their leader tried to stand a little taller, but still grimaced, "And how do you defeat a wind whisperer?"

His friend looked at the ground as he spoke softly, "You don't."

Joe and Elaine walked out into the sunlit courtyard, paused near a bench, and she gestured for them to sit facing the woods. She asked him, tentatively, "What was all that about?"

He reached out his hand, which she took, and he took a slow deep breath. "This will be a long story. How much time do you have?"

She looked intensely into his eyes, "As long as it takes."

He took her hand in both of his, "You know that I began taking Hebrew last year?" She nodded. "Well, about six months ago, a guest lecturer spoke about an ancient book of Hebrew poetry called the Beharuach. He invited me to join a small study group and has used that book of Hebrew mystical poetry to teach me the intricacies of the language. I had studied Hebrew in high school at a local synagogue by special permission, to fulfill my language requirement, so, the basics of the language came back to me quite quickly, but it is more a language of flavored nuances than of structured syntax." He stopped for a moment, "Am I boring you?"

Elaine smiled and looked down at the hand he held, "No, not at all. However, I might find it easier to concentrate if you let go of my hand."

He had forgotten that he was holding it. He reluctantly let go and continued. "The lecturer taught that through words one must maintain the vital and life giving connection to the wind or Spirit." He paused again to let the words sink in. "As you know there were two trees in the garden of Eden, the tree of Knowing and the Tree of Life. It was not that the one tree was good and the other bad, but that eating of the tree of Knowing was prohibited if sought apart from God Himself. The Tree of Life was seen more as a personification of God Himself and not separate from Him. The Tree of Life might also be translated the Tree of Breath, or the Tree of the Wind. Therefore, as part of our study of Hebrew and the Beharuach, the lecturer, a Rabbi Levi Shammah, later introduced me to the Tree of the Wind. His name is Chayeem."

She squinted, "You mean as though he was a person."

He grinned, "Yes, exactly because He is a person."

She looked a little sideways at him, "You're kidding?"

He shook his head slightly, "No, I am quite serious."

"How?" she barely whispered.

"Well, it might seem a little complicated, but bear with me. It really is quite simple. When man and woman did wrong and had to leave the Garden, God began a process that would allow them to return. That process is a person, Jesus. Where the Tree Chayeem was a personification of God, Jesus is God in human form, or He was back then. He died to take away the wrong that stands between you and God, and lives to restore your relationship to God. You simply have to ask Him to do it for you."

She asked again, "How?"

"Just talk to Him as though He was here, because He is."

She grinned slightly, "Why can't I see Him?"

"You can't see the wind either, or electricity, but you believe in them," he stated matter-of-factly. "Just ask Jesus to remove your wrong and restore your relationship to God."

She felt foolish talking to someone she couldn't see, but she tried anyway, "Jesus, please take away the wrong that stands between me and God." She paused for a minute, looking at Joe, who nodded, "and restore my relationship with You both," and she waited. Suddenly her countenance changed as an almost tangible feeling of awe and beauty poured into her very being. She gasped, "Is that Him?"

Joe replied, "From the look on your face, I would say that there's a pretty good chance that, yes, that's Him."

Tears filled her eyes and she sobbed softly for a few minutes. When she was done, Joe announced, "Now that you are connected to the Spirit, the wind, He can share with you His words for things. Ask him to share with you a word."

She took a slow deep breath, "Please share with me a word." Joe watched her face. Initially she looked puzzled, then she did not.

So, he asked, "What did He share with you?"

She spoke softly, reverently, "Gilboah."

"A bubbling fountain," Joe translated.

She met his gaze with surprise, "Yes! I saw a picture of water bubbling about ten inches out of the ground and people flocking to it."

It was Joe's turn to take a slow deep breath. He began, "Place your hands over your heart and whisper that word softly and slowly with me, "Gilboah." She did as he asked and joined him in whispering the word. "Again, Gilboah." Each time her eyes got wider as she felt something profoundly occurring deep within her soul and spirit. "You see, Elaine, you are Gilboah. You are that bubbling spring that will provide what is lacking to those who are truly seeking. This is being established in you, here and now." A tear had formed in the corner of her eye. As it drifted down her cheek, she knew he spoke the truth. She had whispered her first word and things would never be the same.

Chapter Seven
Rabbi Levi Shammah

Joe sat alone with Rabbi Shammah after the rest of the study group had left the class. "Rabbi, I recently introduced a friend of mine to Jesus, the Messiah, may she join us?"

Levi smiled, "When we are no longer in class you can just call me Levi."

Joe frowned, "That doesn't seem appropriate…Rabbi." Joe was confused.

Levi was still smiling, "I guess it would depend on the nature of your question. Are you seeking a rabbinic answer or the answer of a friend? She wants to study Beharuach?"

Joe looked over Levi's right shoulder then back into his eyes, "No, I think she just needs the fellowship of others who know Jesus as the Messiah."

"As a friend then, I think you can invite her to join us when we meet on the Sabbath. Does that answer your question?" Levi still smiled.

A small grin touched Joe's face, "I think so."

Levi responded, "Let me ask you a question, what does Messiah mean?'"

Joe could answer that easily, "It means anointed, empowered."

Levi laid the palm of his right hand on his copy of the Beharuach, "Go deeper."

Joe looked down at the table and closed his eyes. He saw a picture of a candle being lit in the darkness as he whispered the word that had come to him.

Levi awoke him out of his reverie, "Are we not all called to a special purpose?"

Joe took a slow deep breath as he looked up from the table, "Yes, but we are not all Jesus."

Levi chuckled, "Yes, Jesus was 'specialer,'" and he paused a moment, then continued, "I like that word, 'specialer'... but the truth of the matter is that we are called to be saints or to be holy ones, because we too are called out of the commonness of this world and into a special purpose. He did say that we are the light of the world. Perhaps not in the same way that He is, but in a similar way."

"Ahh, I think I am beginning to get it." Joe looked back into Levi's eyes.

"Good! So, your friend is more than welcome to join us on the Sabbath and begin to learn about her specialness," and he sighed contentedly.

Again, seated at the dining hall, Joe brought up the subject, "So, having met the King of the Universe, what do you think?"

She looked shyly down at the table, "I'm not sure what I expected, but it was not this."

"Meaning?"

"It seems that He likes me and enjoys spending time with me," she struggled finding the right words. "I thought He'd be more aloof and god-like."

"But it's still wonderful?" Joe asked.

She sighed, "Yes."

"Would you be interested in meeting with some of us who have a similar experience, but have been with Him longer?" He wasn't sure how she'd respond. Maybe she would feel intimidated.

She had been looking away. She looked back, "Yes, I would."

He looked away himself, "It will probably be a bit different than you might expect."

"How so?"

"Well," he began, "we meet on Saturdays, the Sabbath." He looked back for a reaction, but if there was one it was more anticipation than surprise, "And it has a lot of Jewish or Hebrew flavor to it."

She grinned, "Like leeks and garlic?"

He grinned too, "No, the music, the dancing."

She interrupted, "You dance?" Now she was surprised.

He went on, "Yes, but more all together, Hebrew-like."

She looked surprised, but pleased. "This is beginning to sound like fun."

Joe relaxed, "It is, but there are some more serious times as Rabbi Shammah shares with us out of the Scriptures."

"Old Testament, New Testament..." she left her sentence incomplete.

"Yes, and some other scriptures that are extra Biblical."

She blanched a little at that, "You're not a cult are you?"

He chuckled, "No, no, no, nothing like that. They are just sources that you would be unfamiliar with."

She interjected, "Like the Beharuach?"

He lifted his shoulders, "Well, sort of like that, I guess. Still interested?"

She was. "Yes, when will you pick me up?"

Joe sounded relieved, "Well, since it's about a ten minute walk from the campus, I'll stop by your dorm at about nine thirty-five."

"Are slacks okay?"

"Yes, we are mostly college-age folk. I will be dressed in business casual."

"Okay, it's a date!" The 'date' part was in jest.

The rest of their lunch seemed less intense.

"He was right," she thought, *"This is interesting, different, and sort of fun."* They had just finished a number of pretty raucous songs and a couple of dances. They were meeting in the large basement of a luxurious home. Someone was cooking upstairs, it filtered downstairs, and it smelled wonderful. The final song was soft, slow, and more contemplative. There were chairs stacked up against the walls of the room. When they were done with that final song, everybody walked to the wall, picked up a chair, moved to the middle of the room, and sat in it. Elaine, watching them all, did the same. The thirty or so of them formed a large circle, leaving a spot for the Rabbi and his chair. One of the group prayed. Elaine noticed that no one bowed their head nor closed their eyes. It was just as though the person praying was speaking to someone else right there in the room. Although strange, it was rather intimate.

Up until this moment it had just seemed like a college group that sang and danced, but things became somber and expectant during prayer. Rabbi Shammah entered and also sat.

He spoke with a bit of an accent, as though English was not his native language. "Anyone have something they feel that they would like to share with us?"

One of the gals, in a group of six of them, stood up, "We have a couple visitors with us this morning. I'm Francine, although I go by Fran. This last week my cat died. I know, he was just a cat, but I found him when he was a kitten, and I was even able to move him with me to college because we live off campus." The rest of the gals were looking at the floor. "My friends," and she gestured around her "all fell in love with him. He's the only guy we ever knew that we were sure we could trust." She laughed slightly and one of the guys called out, "Come on, that's unfair." It did lighten the mood a little, then Fran continued, "We all really miss him. I miss him. I come home from class and I expect him to greet me at the door, but all that greets me is emptiness." Now, she looked down at the floor too.

Joe spoke up, but didn't stand, "I know to say that your cat is in a better place seems trite, but that makes it nonetheless true."

Fran looked up at Joe and then at the Rabbi, "You mean there really is a cat heaven?"

Rabbi Shaman gestured to Joe, "Yes, in Ecclesiastes, the third chapter, it says that men and beasts have the same breath. The word that he uses for breath is the word for spirit or wind and we are all familiar with who the Tree of the Wind is. The one place he is referring to is more than dust to dust because he later says, 'Who knows whether the spirit of man goes upward and the spirit of the beast goes down into the earth?' I would translate that, 'Is there a heaven for humans and a heaven for cats?' No one knows for sure, but I would lean towards one heaven, just for economy's sake. Regardless, the spirit is eternal, it does not die. The spirit of your cat lives on and I'm pretty sure that you will see him again."

Fran had begun to weep softly and those next to her had put their hands on her shoulders. Joe then spoke out, "Would You," and he looked upward, "please take these words that You had recorded in Ecclesiastes and plant them deep in Fran's heart and those of her friends." Although Joe had not said "Amen," a number of others did.

Fran dried her eyes, looked up to Joe, and mouthed, "Thank you."

Chapter Eight
The Rabbi Speaks

"And thank you, Fran," Rabbi Shammah added and paused. Then he began, "The Apostle Paul wrote to Timothy,

> *All scripture is given by inspiration, and is profitable for doctrine, for reproof, for correction, and for instruction in righteousness.*

It is an interesting passage and I'd like to begin unpacking it a little. The word used for inspiration is 'God-breathed.' It is as though God is the breath behind the speaking of the words. Remember, many of the Scriptures (like the gospels) were first transmitted orally and only later written down. Next, the word translated 'scripture' is simply 'writing.' Does that mean that everything that is written is inspired? I suppose that in some sense it is, yes, but not all writing is inspired in the same way or for the same purpose. If I write a book, I can speak about how I was inspired to write it. A beautiful sunset might inspire a few verses of poetry, but here we are looking at writing that is inspired to teach us, correct us, and be a guide to righteous living. That's a little different than a pretty sunset. Give us an example of inspired writing." Allen raised his hand, "Al?"

Allen smiled, "The Torah, the first five books of Moses."

Rabbi Shammah gestured towards Joe, "And Ecclesiastes?"

It was Joe's turn to smile, "Yes, but I would probably not want to build my life on, 'Vanity, vanity, all is vanity, a striving after the wind.'"

There were chuckles around the room, but Rabbi Shammah lifted a finger, "Ah, but with our understanding of the Wind, is He not worth all of our striving after Him?" He lifted his finger heavenward.

Joe gestured towards the Rabbi with both his hands, palms up, "Point taken."

Rabbi Shammah took a slow deep breath, "Most of us begin our day devotionally. Why?"

Marion spoke out, "It's like starting the race with our feet firmly planted in the starting blocks rather than aimlessly wandering around the starting line." She was a runner and many of her examples came from running.

"Yes, it sets our day in proper order. When you dive under water, do you take a breath before or after you dive in?" Alex raised his hand. "I think I asked that rhetorically, but thanks, Alex," Rabbi Shammah responded. Alex lowered his hand. "When we begin our day breathing properly, there is a better chance that we can maintain that breathing throughout the day."

Rabbi Shammah brought out another book and held it up, "What is this?"

Doris, who sat nearest him said, "The Book of Mormon."

He grinned, "Is it scripture?"

Doris added, "It definitely qualifies as writing?" And she chuckled before she continued, "The Church of Jesus Christ of Latter Day Saints would say, 'Yes, it is inspired.' The question would then become, 'How inspired is it?'"

Rabbi picked it up from there, "The Latter Day Saints would say it is profitable for doctrine, teaching, correction, etc. They do not say it replaces the Torah, or is equal to it, but call it 'another Testament to Jesus Christ.' How many of you have read it?" Dwayne raised his hand. "What did you think?"

He seemed a little hesitant to respond, as though put on the spot, "A friend of mine challenged me to read it. I was reluctant, but he told me to pretend it was just a novel. I did and found it quite interesting. I have read it a couple of times now and it has proved useful as I have developed some LDS friendships. It means a lot to them that you have read their special book."

Rabbi Shammah was nodding his head, "Yes it does." He looked around the group. "I would encourage you all to read it, not instead of the Old and New Testament, but...." and he paused grinning again, "as a novel. It will take you awhile, it is a little over five hundred pages long." He looked at Fred, "And don't just skim it, but really read it carefully." He chuckled, "There'll be a test on it next month. Just kidding, but do read it carefully. It might matter." He looked around the group again, "Any questions?"

Fred leaned forward, "Don't the Mormons have some weird beliefs?"

Rabbi Shammah thought a moment, "First off, they prefer to no longer be referred to as Mormons, too many negative connotations. But then I have heard that you, Fred, have some weird beliefs." Fred's eyes widened, "Don't worry, I won't expose you in front of everyone."

Fred spoke again, "But I've heard they believe in a different Jesus."

"Hmmm," Rabbi Shammah intoned, "heard.... that would be called 'hearsay.' Is hearsay admissible in court?"

Fred looked at the floor, "No sir."

"Then, again, I would suggest you read it and see for yourself."

Still trying to redeem himself, Fred countered, "But I don't need to read 'Playboy' to know that I shouldn't."

Rabbi Shaman laughed out loud, """I don't think the problem with Playboy lies in your reading it. I think it has something to do with your motivation, your reason for reading it." A few chuckles erupted in the group. "While there are usually some pictures in the 'Book of Mormon' I can assure you that none of them contain scantily clad women." Fred finally cut his losses and leaned back.

Any other questions?" There were none, "Okay, Fred, could you close our time in prayer," and the Rabbi chuckled again, "without betraying any of your funny beliefs?" Fred did and they got up to greet one another before going upstairs for supper.

Chapter Nine
Nurse and Systems Analyst

Quite a lot happened during the last two years of school. Joe began his job as a Systems Analyst for Dragoon Software, working thirty-two hours a week, while still taking a full load at John Wesley. Elaine began the nursing portion of her education which now contained her clinical training in a local hospital. That left little time for romance, yet they still kept the fires burning. With only six months of school left, Joe finally popped the question, and she had provisionally accepted.

She shared her terms, "My acceptance of this proposal is contingent on success in two areas. The first would be the ring. You are not getting a firm 'Yes' from me without a ring. Second, is my father's blessing. That may be some what more difficult than acquiring the ring."

Joe's 'gulp' was audible, but he said that he would do his best over the weekend. He met with Elaine's father alone. Her father upstaged Joe with, "If it's about asking for the hand of my daughter in marriage," and he paused to let Joe sweat a little, "the answer is Yes." Her mother and I have expected this for a while and have prayed about it. I have some other good news for you." He left the room to return with Elaine's mother.

She handed him a small box as she said, "That's my mother's ring. I have had it sized for Elaine's finger. She doesn't know about it, so it will still be a surprise." Joe nearly cried.

Sunday afternoon he proposed, but this time with her father's blessing and her grandmother's ring. She said, "Yes," and even let him kiss her, chastely. They began planning a small wedding after graduation, in her parent's Baptist church.

The wedding was a small intimate affair with just her parents, a few of Elaine's friends and some members of the church. They honeymooned at a small motel near a lake. Their first night was the 'first' for both of them. It was slow, tender, and wonderful. They set up house in a one bedroom apartment that Joe had located. It was between the hospital where Elaine now worked and the offices of Dragoon Software.

They soon settled into their marriage routine. Elaine worked second shift at the hospital. Being new, she had to start at the bottom and work her way up to the better schedules. The day shift was not necessarily preferable amidst all the craziness, especially that of having to deal with all the egotistical doctors. Second shift was much more laid back and many of the nurses had worked there for years because of that very fact. She fit in well and soon became accepted by all the staff.

She worked on a surgical ward, so there was plenty of work to do between preparing patients for their surgery the next day, to taking care of those who had just come out of surgery, to encouraging those who found the painlessness of anesthesia was being eclipsed by the results of their surgery. She learned early that it was best to keep her patients ahead of their pain by providing regular doses at the maximum level of their pain medication, then to slowly reduce the medication until they could transition to less drastic measures. She seemed to have almost a sixth sense about how much pain medication a patient really needed that allowed her to transition her patients much more quickly than others. She became so successful that doctors began to ask her opinion and defer to her judgement.

Meanwhile, Joe had demonstrated his value at Dragoon Software. After the honeymoon, he transitioned to full-time. Dragoon had built its brand name and reputation on having produced the best transcription software available on the Windows platform, but it faced two huge problems. First, it was voice dependent. To achieve better than a ninety-five percent word recognition during the transcription process required a significant investment of time to train the software to recognize each individual user's voice. Secondly, it was platform dependent. It currently only ran on a Windows-based system. Joe stepped up to lead a number of focus groups. In Question and Answer sessions he determined that before they concentrated on migrating the software to other platforms it was more important to the users that they develop an independent version. The list of requirements that resulted from his focus groups so impressed the management team that they they forwarded it to upper management. They were looking for a team to turn those requirements into the code that fulfilled them.

Joe entered the office of the Vice President of Development with a mixture of awe and trepidation. Julius Ridgmore was a legend in the industry. He had led a team that had completed the most successful migration of CPM data to the MS-DOS environment on the planet. That move had saved the bacon of many large and small companies and had cemented the value of IT departments all over the country. Dragoon's "Plain Speaking" had been his brainchild and with a lot of blood, sweat, and long hours they had launched this new and revolutionary piece of transcription software.

"Joe, have a seat," and Mr. Ridgmore pointed to one of the seats on the other side of his desk.

"Yes, sir," Joe replied.

"You don't have to address me as, 'Sir'. JR will do just fine," JR lightly chuckled.

"Yes…JR," Joe stammered.

"Your name has come across my desk a number of times since you started with us," he looked down at his notes, "two years ago?" Joe nodded. "I was also very impressed with the requirements document that you brought back to us from your Q&A sessions." Joe smiled a bit sheepishly, embarrassed. " How would you like to lead the team that turns those requirements into reality?"

Joe was shocked, "Really?"

JR smiled slightly, "You should know that I rarely joke. I believe humor is important, but I am much more impressed with results and you deliver!"

Joe let it sink in a moment before he responded, "Thank you…. JR." He had difficulty calling him that. It seemed too personal.

JR continued, "So would you like to lead the team?"

Joe took a deep breath, "Yes, I would indeed."

"I'll give you a day to draw up your requirements for personnel, equipment, etc. Schedule a meeting with my secretary for the following day and then meetings with HR and IT for the day after that. By the end of next week I would like a preliminary schedule that we can hammer into reality. Have a great day." He looked down at his schedule.

Joe, dismissed, got up and turned to leave, with a, "Thank you again…JR." He left smiling to himself.

The next day, Joe presented JR with his requirements. He looked them over quickly and then signed the sheet of paper as he asked, "Do you have an appointment with HR and IT?"

Joe smiled, "Yes, one after the other beginning in about ten minutes."

JR smiled too, "So, you didn't think I'd fuss over your requirements?"

Joe's smile remained, "Review them, yes, fuss over them, no."

JR chuckled, "I knew I picked the right guy! Off you go!" Joe reached out his hand which JR shook as they both stood. Joe turned and left for his meeting with HR.

Chapter Ten
Meeting HR and IT

His sheet of requirements with JR's signature was treated like the Holy Grail. Joe was quickly escorted to an office by Anita, an HR Specialist. "So, Joe, explain these requirements to me a little more," as she pointed to a chair on the other side of her desk.

Joe sat, "I'm building a team for a rather important project. Those are the categories and some of the skills I need. I'm looking for effectiveness over experience. I'd like these individuals to be in the top ten percent on their last employee evaluation."

Anita had gotten up and moved around to sit next to him. She set her laptop on the table behind them and they both turned towards the table. She created a list of those who had scored in the top ten percent of their last employee evaluation. She sorted them by specialty and ranked them by score.

Joe inquired, "Can I have access to their folders?"

Anita looked at JR's signature, thought a moment, then replied, "I can arrange for limited access that will allow you to see what you need, yet still protect their privacy."

Joe added, "Can I have it this afternoon?"

"Just a minute," and Anita started typing the keys on her laptop. Her fingers flew over the keyboard. Joe sat there patiently. "There, you have it. I have added some boxes for you to check as you review them. Among them are 'rejected,' 'add to the team,' and 'requires further review.' The folder of anyone that you reject will no longer be available to you. How does that sound?"

Joe reached out his hand. She shook it as he said, "That's wonderful. You have been a great help."

"The next time you log on there will be an option Potential Team Members that you can open. Once you do, it will take you to the folders, sorted by specialty. Will that be okay?" She was proud of her ability to help him.

He was appreciative, "Yup, great!"

"Anything else you need, you have my number and email." She got up and Joe did too.

He smiled, "I'm off to IT. I hope they are as helpful. Thanks again."

The IT department also treated Joe's requirement's letter, signed by JR, as the Holy Grail. He was given assurances that whatever he needed would be supplied in short order. In the interim, they gave him the layout of some office space that he could use as the home for his new team. Joe would call it the "IUSR," the "Independent User Speach Recognition" team and he went back to his desk prepared to design and build their own little kingdom.

Joe looked slowly through the folders that Anita had sent him. He rejected a number of them on that first pass. He took copious notes on the others. He went through the folders a second time revising his initial impressions. He went through them a final time and settled on six team members. The first was Nate Dover, a database specialist. His evaluation was stellar and his results spectacular. Next was Ted Rogers, an expert in the development of search engines. One comment in particular had caught his attention, "Ted's ability to weave requirements together to identify the exact result we were looking for has impressed us repeatedly." Then there was David Timmons, a systems analyst like Joe himself. His addition to the team would support turning the requirements into a finished product and he might be able to act as Joe's second in command. Finally there was the coding team of Carl Nordling, Janice Woodrum, and Elise Granger. Joe sent the list to Anita and made an appointment with her for the following day.

They both sat again at the table in her office as she brought his team folders up one at a time. "Wow," she said. "You picked some really top notch people." Joe let a little smile grace his face. "Nate was the most difficult for me to get. Fortunately, we had that letter signed by JR. Nate's boss wasn't willing to put his own job on the line to keep Nate working for him. Ted and David had just completed assignments, so we asked for them at an opportune moment." That was half of the team. "The manager of the coders is a bit of an arrogant fellow, in my opinion. He said, 'Take whomever you want. Coders are a dime a dozen.' I don't think he had any idea of the true value of Carl and Janice." Joe breathed a sigh of relief. Anita followed with, "Elise was a bit of a surprise. She's both young and new to us. I'm curious, why did you pick her?"

Joe had his hands folded in his lap. He placed the right one flat on the table, "That's exactly why I picked her. Her community college scores were great. She will add a freshness and vitality to the team. She's also probably hungrier than the rest. I think she will help light a fire under all of them. At least, that's what I'm hoping."

Anita was nodding her assent, "I can see why JR picked you."

Joe had folded his hands on the table. It reminded Anita of someone about to pray. He said, "I have one more request. It might be a little unorthodox. I'd like to offer each of them the opportunity personally. I want it to be their choice, not just an assignment they have to take. Is that okay?"

Anita wasn't sure that she could be more surprised, but she was. "Ah, sure. Their management has been notified, so we are clear there. I'm not sure what they have told their employees, but," she paused, "go for it and good luck."

Joe returned, "I don't believe in luck, I believe in creating opportunity." He reached over and shook her hand, "Thanks again."

Anita's eyes followed him as he left her room. *"That one will bear watching,"* she mused.

Chapter Eleven
Thursday at Dragoon

Joe waited long enough until each of his team members were probably settled into their day and then he went and found the first one, David, his systems analyst. First, Joe found his department, located his desk, then approached him. Joe was good with names and faces, mostly because he worked at it. He knew that calling you by your name was the second most loving thing he could say to you. The only more loving thing was to say, "I love you," and that was not appropriate at work. Connect the face to the name and you had a powerful relational tool.

David had his head buried in a three-ring binder when Joe stepped up to his desk.

"David," his tone was friendly and David looked up neither startled nor surprised. Joe had his hand extended, "Joe Huddleston, could we go for a walk?"

Now he was a bit surprised, "Sure," and he started to get up from his desk. There was an atrium on that floor and they walked to it.

Joe gestured to a chair, David sat and so did Joe, "Do you go by Dave or David?"

David smiled, "David would be great, thanks for asking."

Joe found himself liking him already. "I'm forming a team to take our speech recognition software to the next level. I want you to be on that team."

Now David was fully surprised. "Really?"

Joe smiled too, "Yes, really. HR has talked to your management and they will release you, but this is not an assignment. I want it to be your choice." David's eyes widened a little more. "Here's the requirements document and my contact information. Take a look at it and let me know today or tomorrow. If you decide, yes, you will report to me on Monday."

David chuckled, "More money?"

Joe chuckled in return, "Not initially, but when we pull this off, I think the sky will be the limit."

David answered a little more seriously, "Well, your timing is spot on. I just finished a project. I'll try and get back to you today."

Joe stood and reached out his hand. "Email, text, or call me with your decision." He handed him his card.

David shook Joe's hand, "You got it."

Joe turned and walked away. David sat and began going through the requirements document.

Next on his list was Nate, the database specialist. Nate looked up as Joe approached his desk. Joe stuck out his hand, "Nate, Joe Huddleston." Joe liked that Nate got out of his chair to shake Joe's hand. "Could we take a walk?"

Nate looked around as he said, "And you are?"

Joe looked serious as he said, "Ethics," then laughed, "Not really. Come on, I promise it won't hurt."

Nate looked around again like, "*Is this really okay*?" Then started around his desk as Joe began to turn and go.

This floor had its own coffee shop, so they went there. Joe pointed to a chair, "Cup of coffee? My treat," which was funny also because the coffee was free.

Nate shook his head as he smiled, "Tea, Earl Grey."

Joe went to the counter and returned with his decaf and Nate's tea. He sat down.

Nate ventured, "So, what's this all about?"

Joe gave his spiel and left Nate with a copy of the requirements.

Joe then had to video call Ted who was working from home. That put a bit of a damper on his presentation and he had to email him the requirements document, but the video chat seemed to go okay.

The three coders all worked in the same area, so Joe had reserved their conference room for an hour. He brought Janice in and explained things to her. Then he brought in Carl. Last, he brought in Elise.

"Elise, my name is Joe Huddleston," and he reached out his hand. She looked at it for a minute and then shook it, albeit tentatively. "I've heard great things about you, have a seat," and he pointed to a chair at the corner of the conference table. She sat and he sat around the corner from her.

"What's this all about? I saw you speak with Janice and Carl, but couldn't tell their reaction as they left the room."

"Well, I made them an offer, but it's their choice, as it is yours. I'm starting up a new team to take our speech recognition software to the next level and I want the three of you on the team." He tried to be upbeat and confident, and he usually succeeded.

"They're pretty senior members of the coding team here, why me?" she asked cautiously.

"That's true, they are, but I believe your youth and passion will add a needed ingredient to the team." He smiled warmly.

She still seemed less than convinced. "Who else do you have on the team?"

Joe sighed, "A database specialist, a systems analyst, and a search engine expert," although none of them were confirmed yet.

"And this is not an assignment, I don't have to do this?" She questioned.

"Nope, read the requirements document," and he put it on the table in front of her, "talk with Janice and Carl, and let me know. I'd like your decision today or tomorrow."

"That's a pretty quick decision." she still treaded softly. "How long will the project take?"

"You would report to me Monday and I want to take the project's schedule to the Vice President that Friday. Can you get back to me by tomorrow?"

"If I say no, can you get by with just two coders?" She had him over a barrel.

He looked off to the right, thinking, "Nope, I'd have to find someone else over the weekend."

Elise relaxed, "I like you, Joe. Count me in."

Joe was shocked, "You haven't looked at the requirements!"

She smiled, "They don't matter. As I'm sure you have heard, 'Coders are just coders, dime a dozen.' What matters to me is who I work with. Janice and Carl are two of the best. That, and I like your style. I think I will enjoy working with you."

She got up even before he did, grabbed the document in her left hand and reached out her right. Joe stood and she shook his hand this time firmly, "See you Monday!"

He stood there a minute and by the time he left the conference room he noticed the three of them huddled around Janice's desk discussing the requirements document.

Chapter Twelve
Another Late Dinner

Joe returned home late, but well satisfied with the results of his day. By Monday he would be heading up a new team that could significantly alter the position of their product. If they were able to successfully bring the first independent speech recognition software to market it would establish them as a new premier product for years to come. Elaine, working swing shift, wouldn't be home until almost midnight. He would have to wait to share his big day until then. He had brought home a couple of pizzas and taken a short nap before she got there.

He gave her a chance to speak first, "How was your day?"

"Funny that you should ask," she began, "the orderly was walking Mr. Dawson down the hallway when he suddenly collapsed in the orderly's arms. We ran a wheelchair out to him, got him back to his room and on his bed. He was dead. We started CPR on him and called a code. By the time the crash cart got there the orderly and I had brought him back to life, although I'm pretty sure the orderly broke a couple of ribs. If you don't break a couple of ribs, you probably aren't doing CPR strong enough, but I have had enough of kissing an old dead man for awhile." She winked at him.

Joe looked down at his cold pizza, "I guess that sort of eclipses my day," he paused, "saving a man's life." He paused again, "I wouldn't say Dragoon Software is dead, but if I don't breathe life into its premier speech recognition application, it might be. I have been given the privilege of leading a team that will take it to the next level. We will make it user voice independent. That means that no longer will you have to go through extensive training to get the software application to recognize ninety-five percent of your words. No, it will do so, without hardly any training whatsoever, nearly right out of the box."

She furrowed her brows, "Is that even possible?"

Joe smiled and reached out his hand, which she took, "No, and bumble bees can't fly, and you can't bring back people to life who have died." Elaine smiled back.

"JR, the vice president of software development, was impressed with the results of my Question and Answer focus groups and the list of requirements that I extracted from those meeting." He took a breath, his excitement building, "He gave me the charter to form a team to turn those requirements into the new functionality of our speech recognition app. I will have six specialists in the different aspects of it reporting to me on Monday."

"Saving a life is a wonderful thing, but it probably won't translate into increased income," she noted. "Reviving Dragoon software though may do exactly that!" She took another piece of pizza.

Joe took a deep breath, "I just hope it's going to be worth all the long hours I'm afraid it will require, and at the end of it all we'll still be friends."

Elaine laughed, "I don't think we have to worry very much about that," and she lovingly punched him in the shoulder. "Maybe it's time we started trying to have a family?"

Joe looked surprised, "I thought we already were a family."

She winked at him, "You know what I mean."

He winked back at her, "Then you better hurry up and finish that pizza, time's a wasting."

She smiled slyly, "You finish cleaning up while I finish this piece of pizza. Then I'll race you to the bedroom." She took another bite as he put their plates and cups in the dishwasher.

He kept looking back over his shoulder, "No head starts!"

Chapter Thirteen
Elise

Elise Ginger was the daughter of parents addicted to a highly virulent strain of the Chinese drug whose street name was "Crutch." However, Elise was lucky to be born drug free, during the only time her mother was clean and sober. Elise's conception, the pregnancy, and her delivery were all done when her mother was drug free. Her mother then went back on the drugs to combat her postpartum blues. The neglect of their baby daughter resulted in Elise being taken by CPS and shopped to a number of foster homes, some of which were abusive. When she was fourteen, she left her currently abusive home and took to the local streets. Fortunately, she wasn't out there very long before an elderly gentleman, Stephen, found her and asked her if she wanted some breakfast that morning.

Elise looked deeply into his eyes. They were the softest blue she had ever seen. "I haven't eaten since last night," she confessed.

Stephen pointed, "Then, may I take you to that restaurant and buy you some breakfast?"

She had continued watching his eyes closely, "Sure." They walked over and entered the restaurant. The hostess sat them at a booth in the back corner and handed them each a menu. A few minutes later the waitress joined them.

Stephen smiled, "I usually have the $6.99 sausage, eggs, and pancakes," he addressed Elise, "but you can have whatever you'd like."

The waitress, Sue, asked, "Your usual?" and Stephen nodded. She looked at Elise.

She studied the menu a moment longer then said, "A small stack of pancakes and a side of two eggs, sunny-side up." She paused, then added, "please."

The waitress nodded, "And to drink?"

Stephen responded, "Coffee, cream and sugar."

Elise looked at Stephen, "Hot chocolate?"

"Of course," Stephen said as he looked to the waitress. She hadn't written anything down. She never did, she just relied on remembering all of it. Stephen got up to use the restroom and when he returned Sue had brought them their drinks.

As they conversed, Elise realized that Stephen was familiar with most of the haunts that she currently frequented. She wondered if he made it his business to help people in distress. *"Hmmm, something to think about."* He sure did seem to be compassionate, and caring, and the pancakes were delicious. They had come with a variety tray of syrups. She had eaten her eggs, sopped up their remains with some toast and then started on the pancakes. She tried three of the different syrups and still wasn't sure which one she liked the best. She had difficulty believing how easy it was to talk to Stephen. She had never met anyone quite like him. The waitress came and cleared away their dishes and Stephen took a refill of his coffee. Elise was content to sit there and nurse her hot chocolate.

The restaurant door open and Stephen quietly exclaimed, "Oh good, Dan and Doris." A couple about Stephen's age waved and came over to their table.

Dan reached out his hand towards Elise, "Dan," then looking at Stephen, "would it be okay if we joined you?"

Elise looked at Stephen as she said, "Elise," Stephen raised his eyebrows and Elise responded, "Sure." They sat down and the waitress came with their menus.

They handed the menus right back to her, "Our usual please, Sue."

Sue smiled, "I should have known," and left them.

Dan smiled and it seemed to warm the very atmosphere, "So, Elise, what brings you to breakfast with Stephen?"

She felt like she could tell them anything and began. She was only interrupted when Dan and Doris' drinks and later their food were brought to the table. Dan and Doris listened intently. Finally she ended with, "and how long have you known Stephen?" She probably should have asked that sooner, but she got carried away with their attention to her story.

Doris answered this time, "We have know Stephen for a long time. As you have experienced, he finds young people who are out on their own and when suitable, introduces them to us. Over the years, we have helped a number of them join society as contributing adults." She paused and looked at Dan, who nodded. "This may sound a little strange, but how would you like to come and live with us until you find your," he paused, "feet?"

She looked at Doris, Dan, and then at Stephen who nodded. Tears began to form in the corners of her eyes, "You would do that? After listening to my story, you would let me come and live with you?"

Dan responded, "We have Stephen's recommendation too."

She looked at Stephen, who nodded again, "But he has only known me a little longer than you." And she looked back at Dan.

Dan smiled, "Stephen does his research. We have never been disappointed at his recommendation and we have had many."

Elise took a long slow breath, "I suppose it wouldn't hurt to go look at your place."

Dan and Doris had finished their plate and Stephen caught the waitress' attention, "Just a single check for all of us and I'll get it."

Dan, Doris, and Elise expressed their thanks as they got up to go, turned, and left the restaurant. Doris had her arm around Elise's shoulder by then.

Sue brought the check, Stephen looked at it, handed her some money with a, "Keep the change and I'll have one final cup of coffee." She came right back to fill his cup and he sat there in the satisfaction of how well that all went.

Elise found Dan and Doris' home a sanctuary, a place of serenity from all the others she had experienced, especially the abusive ones. Here she found help and support. They got her enrolled in classes to fulfill her GED and later helped sponsor her to Junior College. While she attended Junior College she found that she especially excelled at mathematics and programing code. Before she finished the second year she had begun an internship with the local software firm. Although just a small cog in the big wheels of a gigantic machine, she found her time there rewarding and fulfilling.

Chapter Fourteen
Monday with the IUSR

Joe had placed name tents on the desks, his attempt at initial organization of their seating. He had arranged the desks in a circle in the office. His was just another desk in the circle, albeit a little separate from the rest. It was part of what he wanted to convey to the team. "We are all equal here, I'm just a little more equal than you are," and he would chuckle. He hoped that it would set the tone for some incredible collaboration.

Elise arrived first. He thought that she might. "Elise, welcome to IUSR. I've got you over here by me," and he pointed to her desk. Carl and Janice were right behind her and he greeted them similarly. Next was David, then Nate, and finally Ted. "Let's take these first few minutes and go around the room and introduce yourselves to the rest of the team, telling us a little bit about yourselves." Joe pointed to David.

"I'm David, not Dave, and I already am familiar with Carl and Ted. I'm a Systems Analyst, so you can address me as 'Sir,'" and he chuckled. Elise relaxed visibly. "I am married with two children who wonder who the guy is that occasionally has breakfast with them."

"I am Ted and a search engine specialist."

Nate interrupted him, "and highly regarded amongst the Borg Collective," and snickered.

Ted gave Nate a look, "I too am married, but no kids. Who has time for kids? According to the data it takes twenty years before they contribute anything to society, if then." He looked at Joe, "and I'm looking forward to making history on this project!" Joe nodded.

"I'm Nate, a database designer."

It was Ted's turn to interrupt, "Known as 'Data' amongst the Collective. You're not just a database designer, it's rumored your middle initials are DB!" and it was his turn to chuckle.

"I'm single," and he winked at Janice, who shook her head in disbelief at his audacity, "But not very available, considering how much work we will be doing."

"And I am Carl, lead coder in a vast network of coders," and he too snickered, "who are 'a dime a dozen,' or so we're told." He reached out and placed his hand over Nate's, "and I am gay." Nate quickly withdrew his hand from under Carl's, "which means that I am an unusually optimistic sort of fellow, who thinks work should be spelled 'f…u…n'. I too am single, but having way too much 'work,' I mean 'fun,' to be looking for romance."

Janice smiled and it seemed the sun just emerged from behind a cloud. "Janice, worth a bit more than a dime, or I guess it would be a twelfth of a dime, who just loves to create beautiful music on a laptop keyboard. My social life is none of your business, but I'm already having a good time," and her smile was infectious. "I too am looking forward to making history with this project, making the world an easier place to navigate through."

And finally, "Elise, the youngest member of this team and probably the newest to the company, but that means I am eager to help us make our mark and establish us as the 'best of the best' in Dragoon or anywhere else that builds tools for the masses. I too am single," and she winked at Ted who was a bit shocked, "but ready to do whatever it takes to make this happen."

"Thank you Team IUSR," Joe began. "We have before us what seems like an insurmountable task, to make Dragoon's '*Plain Speaking*' software recognize independent user's speech. This is both a challenge and an opportunity. That is why I have assembled the best of the best, to accomplish this project. Now, I'd like us to move to the whiteboard." They all got up from their desks and moved to the chairs in front of the whiteboard. "So, do we have a volunteer to be our scribe?" Elise stepped up to the board, picked up a pen and the eraser, and turned to the others. "Thanks, Elise. I want to conduct a brainstorming session of the roadblocks to independent speech recognition." Elise wrote "Roadblocks" at the top of the board. "Ideas?"

Janice said, "A noisy environment," and Elise began a list below the title with that as the first entry.

Carl added, "Pronunciation."

Nate, "Vocabulary."

Ted, "Tone. I can say something one way and mean one thing, but if I say it another way it means something entirely different."

"Like sarcasm," Joe clarified, "or irony."

Nate responded, "Wouldn't know, I'm not into humor," and he guffawed.

Elise said, "Punctuation," as she added it.

Nate offered, "I might have added 'processing power', but with the latest advances in technology I think that is no longer a problem."

Ted offered a comment, "We may need to limit the speed at which the user would talk or define an optimum rate. Oh, and what about accent?" Elise added "speed" and "accent."

"Okay, that looks like a good start. Which of these would seem to be the easiest to overcome?" Joe asked the group. Elise raised her hand. Joe snickered, "Thanks for raising your hand, Elise, but I think you can just share it."

She looked down at the table, a little embarrassed. "I think we can lessen a noisy environment by simply suggesting the user find an environment that is quiet."

Unsarcastically, Nate added, "That would make things easier." He paused, "We could also suggest a noise cancelling microphone headset."

Carl piped up, "Or even include one in the box."

"Elise, start a column of solutions to the right of the 'Roadblocks' list," Joe suggested. She wrote "Solutions," and then added "quiet environment" and "noise cancelling microphone" across from "Noisy environment" in the first column.

Janice spoke up, "We could add a training video to the package that would demonstrate how to achieve the best results."

Joe thought just a moment. "That's a great idea. Elise, put that above the 'Solutions' header." She did. "Anything else that might mitigate our problems with a noisy environment?"

Ted said, "This might be a little off the wall, but what about a 'white noise' generator? It could cover up some of the ambient noise that you couldn't get away from that is native to the environment regardless."

Joe exclaimed. "Wow, you guys really are the best of the best! We'll come back to this later. Which of the others roadblocks should we start to work on first?"

Janice spoke again, "Accents." There was a general nodding of heads.

"Ok, you can work individually or in group to develop ideas on how we can do that and we will come together again after lunch. If you need anything, just let David know and he'll take care of it. I'll be back after lunch," and Joe walked back to his desk, grabbed his briefcase and headed for the door.

Joe returned after lunch to find the team ready with their discoveries. "Do you want us to stay at our desks or move into the conference room?"

Joe thought a moment then said, "Stay here at your desks." The rest of them nodded their agreement. For the next two hours they shared a variety of approaches to attacking the problem of accents. They prioritized the list and delegated assignments among themselves. Joe thought, "*Teamwork at its finest.*"

Chapter Fifteen
Accents

Sixth months had elapsed since the launch of Joe's IUSR Team and their attack on the problems that accents posed to the company's speech recognition software. They feverishly worked, sometimes night and day, to solve the problem, and were now assembled in JR's huge conference room to provide an update on their progress. Seated around the conference room table were JR and the other vice presidents. At the end of the table sat two projectors. One displayed a page of text, large enough that they could all read it from where they sat. The other was attached to a laptop running a clone of the company's software that Joe's team had been working with. Besides the team, the following people with heavy foreign accents were also present: Fredrick (German), Alfonso (Mexican), Xian (Chinese), Isabella (Italian), Amelia (British), and Celine (French). Joe stood at the white board next to the projected text. The board listed the accents from top to bottom: German, British, Mexican, French, Chinese, and Italian. An underlined space next to it waited for the percent correct that the software would recognize from the spoken text.

Joe addressed his audience, "I think you will be pleased, perhaps even amazed at what you are about to see." He nodded to Fredrick who was wearing the software's new noise cancelling microphone and head phones. Fredrick read the page of text in his heavily accented German voice. Those seated around the table followed along with the text on the screen. Often they looked at Fredrick when they had difficulty understanding the word he said when compared to what they were reading. They then looked at the output of the software to find it had understood him perfectly. When Fredrick finished, David, who sat at the laptop, pressed a few keys and the words of the text and the output of the software were both quickly highlighted, word by word, as they were compared. The result was one hundred percent accuracy. Joe wrote 100 across from the accent "German" on the white board.

Fredrick removed the microphone headset and passed it to Amelia who donned it. She waited for the software to reset to a blank screen and she began to read. A few minutes after she finished Joe wrote another 100 across from British. This continued through all six of the readers. The lowest accuracy score was 98 for Chinese. The table erupted in applause and JR stood.

"That was an incredible presentation, demonstration," and he paused, "I am nearly speechless." He looked around the table, "That would be a first." They all chuckled. "What do you have left?"

Joe smiled, "We have tone, pronunciation, punctuation, and a few others, but accents was the most difficult. We are pretty sure we can have a finished product by the end of the year."

JR looked at his team, "Whatever you need, you have but to ask."

David piped up, "Do we have a satellite office in the Bahamas so we could work from there?" Joe frowned at him and David added, "just kidding."

JR looked around the table again, "If you give a similar presentation by the end of the year, I can assure you each of two weeks in the Bahamas with your plus one, all expenses paid."

The teams' eyes widened and Elise spoke sheepishly, "Can we go back to work now?"

JR smiled, "Please do," and began applauding again. The other vice presidents joined in and all stood.

The team left the room to that standing ovation.

Chapter Sixteen
Job Complete?

It was the Friday before the Thanksgiving holiday and the IUSR team stood again against the wall of JR's conference room as the vice presidents entered and took their seats around the table. JR walked to the front of the table and stood before the screen in front of the two projectors and two laptops.

JR addressed his peers, "It's been a brutal last few months as SuperSoft released its speech recognition software, 'Speaking Softly.' It appeared to do all that our *'Plain Speaking'* did and they have been selling it for significantly less. Today, that all changes." He gestured towards Joe, "Joe?" Joe stood at the head of his team and moved to the head of the table while David took his seat at the keyboard of one laptop and Elise took a seat at the keyboard of the other.

Joe began confidently, "Well? We think we have done it and you are all about to be amazed again. In front of you are some papers that are part of this presentation. *'Plain Speaking'* still requires a little bit of training to get used to your voice, but it is no longer concerned with your accent as you found out last time. We now believe that we have solved the rest of the problems." Joe pointed to the Vice President of Marketing, "Mr. Dobson, would you please turn to the second page of the document and read that paragraph into *'Plain Speaking'*?" Joe walked over and handed him the headset. "You'll notice there are no cumbersome chords connecting the headset to the computer. Our noise cancelling Bluetooth headset will let you walk around the room while you are speaking, anywhere within a thirty foot radius."

Mr. Dobson didn't need to, but he rose from his seat, donned the headset, and began reading. When he was finished, he sat back down.

Surprisingly, the computer spoke back, asking, "Please reread the sentence with the exclamation point."

Mr. Dobson put the headset back on and reread that sentence.

The computer responded, "Thank you,"

Mr. Dobson asked, "Anything else?" as he smiled at David and the laptop, and removed the headset once again.

Joe turned to Mrs. Fredricks, the head of HR, "Could you please pick a random page of text in the presentation?"

She turned a few pages and called out, "Page seven."

"Mr. Dobson, could you turn to page seven and read that page into the microphone of the headset." Joe smiled as he added, "You didn't know you were going to be the star of the show, did you?"

Mr. Dobson shook his head, smiling, donned the headset once again, and read page seven. When he was through, he asked, "Can I remove the headset now?"

Joe smiled, "Certainly," turned to David, "David?"

David clicked a few keys and the computer responded, "Accuracy, ninety-nine percent."

Mrs. Fredricks asked skeptically, "How does *'Plain Speaking'* know the accuracy of what Ed just read?"

"Good question. For the purposes of this demonstration *'Plain Speaking'* has a copy of the text for compare." Joe responded as he nodded his head.

Mrs. Fredricks raised her eyebrows, "Not to question your integrity, but how do we know that you didn't just tell the program to say that?"

Joe smiled broadly, "I take no offense, but with my job on the line?" and he left the question dangling. "Mr. Dobson, could you hand the headset to Mrs. Fredricks." Joe beamed, "I'm sorry to mess up your hair, but could you read any other page?"

Mrs. Fredricks turned a couple of pages, announced, "Page ten," and began reading. As she read, the words were displayed on the screen. When she was finished, she removed the headset and smoothed out her hair.

"Elise, could you display page ten on your projector and send that page to David?" Elise's keyboard clattered as she did.

Soon words at the beginning of page ten were highlighted one by one, as well as those displayed by 'Plain Speaking.' At the end of the page *'Plain Speaking'* announced "Accuracy, ninety-six percent."

Joe added, "That is pretty astounding! Remember, *'Plain Speaking'* has never heard Mrs. Fredricks' voice before and yet was able to recognize her speech at ninety-six percent accuracy. Let's see 'Speaking Softly' match that at any price!"

The vice presidents began to applaud, but JR stood, "Joe, could you and your team wait outside the room for a few minutes and then we will have you back in?"

Joe looked a bit bewildered, but agreed. Elise and David got up from their laptops and the whole team left the conference room.

Outside, Ted asked, "What do you suppose that's all about?"

Joe looked up to his right, thinking as he spoke, "I think they are discussing our trips to the Bahamas," and he chuckled lightly. Only about two minutes elapsed before Mrs. Fredricks opened the door and invited them back in.

JR spoke from his seated position. "Joe, every year at the company's Christmas dinner we announce the winner of that year's Tim-DOS award." He paused for dramatic effect. "This year we would like to give that award to you and your team." Joe was shocked speechless. "We would like you to keep it a secret until it is announced. Can you do that?"

Joe looked at his team. They were all nodding as he answered, "Yes, sir, we can do that."

JR added casually, "And Joe, we'll have another project for you by Monday." He chuckled, "Keep up the great work! You're dismissed."

"Thank you, sir," and they all filed out of the conference room except Joe who hung back for just a minute. With great restraint they refrained from jumping up and down, dancing around, and giving each other high-fives. They waited until they got back to their team office before they broke out in hoops, hollers, and hugs after closing the door.

Elise seemed to hug Joe a little longer than the others, but he attributed that to his being the team leader and her whispering in his ear, "Thank you for believing in me."

He responded with, "As they say at Chick-fil-A, 'My pleasure.'" She let him go, albeit reluctantly. He asked David, "How close are we to being able to release the updated documentation?"

David answered quickly, "We were pretty sure of today's response and I have been burning the midnight oil on it. I can have it ready Monday morning."

"Great! I held back there a minute in the conference room to ask JR a question. He said I could give you all the rest of the day off." Joe looked at David, "Can you still be ready Monday morning?"

David nodded, "Yes."

"Elise, could I speak to you for just a second?" She looked a little surprised. The others gathered what they needed and left the room. "How artistic are you?" he asked her out of the blue.

She lifted her eyebrows, "Ah, actually, I am quite artistic. I paint, draw, and am a decent photographer. Why do you ask?"

He explained, "I'm going to call a meeting with Graphics about a new cover to the revised software and am wondering if you'd like to go with me?"

She still looked surprised. "I'd love to. What are you thinking?"

He took his laptop to the table and she drew up a chair.

He brought up a copy of the cover of their current software. It contained a rather plain-looking man speaking to a woman as he handed her a copy of something written. He then brought up a copy of a page containing a stylized eternity symbol in green on a light blue background. It said, "Plain Speaking" and under that "Now understanding every voice, always" and down in the lower right corner "Newly Revised Version 7." He stated tentatively, "I was thinking something like this."

Elise leaned in close to take it all in, then sat back, "I like it. I like it a lot. It's plain, yet elegant like the code underneath it. It doesn't have a lot of extra bells and whistles, but what it does, it does exceptionally well.

"Good! The meeting is right after lunch. Do you want to have lunch with me in the cafeteria?" he asked.

She responded simply, "Sure," and she slid her chair back from the table.

Graphics was delighted with Joe's ideas for a new cover and thankful for his mockup. They thought they too would have something for JR by close-of-business Monday. Joe walked back to his desk on a cloud. Elise was especially happy to have been included. Her contribution to the meeting had been, "You might want the light blue background to also contain a hint of purple." The Graphics folks looked at her with surprise, thought a moment, and responded with a, "Definitely!"

Joe and Elise entered the office to find Joe's phone blinking with a message. He stepped up to his desk, lifted the phone to his ear, and pushed the button. He turned to face Elise. "I have an eight o'clock meeting Monday with JR. That's probably our next assignment. We'll have a team meeting when I return." She smiled warmly. He returned her smile and added, "Have a great weekend."

She bounced back with a "You, too," grabbed her coat and purse, and left.

Joe sat at his desk and pondered, *"I wonder what's next?"*

Chapter Seventeen
Monday's Assignment

Joe sat out in front of JR's office, in the waiting area next to his secretary. It was just before eight in the morning. She looked at Joe and smiled, "He's ready for you, you may go in." She stood up and opened his door. Joe nodded to her and walked into JR's office.

JR stood behind his desk and reached his hand across it, "Good morning, Joe."

Joe shook his hand, "Good morning, JR."

JR gestured to the chair across the desk from him, "Have a seat." Joe sat down as JR continued, "Again, great job on making Plain Speaking respond to each individual's voice with virtually no training." He paused as Joe beamed. "Now, the next challenge. We want to produce a Spanish version. Not just one that understands the person with a Spanish accent, you've already done that, but a fully Spanish version, written in Spanish, that recognizes Spanish speech, and transcribes it into Spanish text."

Joe took a deep breath. "Can I continue to have my same team?"

JR simply waved the back of his hand at Joe, "and anything else you need."

Joe responded with, "Great! I met with Graphics last Friday. They should have a box design for version seven today, and David should have finished the documentation. If you get production and advertising on board, you can have the new product on the shelves for the Christmas rush."

JR chuckled, "Are you sure that you're not after my job?"

Joe looked shocked, like someone had just slapped him, "No, sir!"

JR continued his chuckle, "I know, I know. It's just the way you think. It reminds me a lot of me when I was your age."

Joe breathed a relief-filled sigh, "Ah, thank you, sir."

JR's smile broadened, "and what have I said about calling me 'sir'?"

Joe responded, "Yes, sir. I mean, yes, JR."

"Okay, bring me back your requirements when you have them," and he stood and reached out his hand again. Joe stood, shook JR's hand, turned, and walked out of his office.

He stood there in his waiting area for a minute trying to get his thoughts together. Spanish. That was going to be a challenge.

He entered his office still looking a bit bewildered. His team members were all at their desks. He walked in and sat on the edge of his own desk. "He wants a Spanish version, a full Spanish version, that recognizes Spanish and transcribes into Spanish."

Ted piped up, "At least we won't have to worry about Spanish syntax from a native Spanish speaker. Does he want us to be able to write Spanish text from a non-native Spanish speaker?"

That caught Joe off-guard. "Hmmm, good question, but one thing at a time. He said I could keep all of you. Are you up to this new task or do you need some time to think about it?"

Ted added, "I'm up for it if we still get to go to the Bahamas."

A round of laughter filled the room as Elise raised her hand, "I'm up for it. I actually speak Spanish."

Janice raised her hand, "I'm up for it, don't speak Spanish, but I think Assembly language code is independent of all other languages." That brought another round of chuckles. The rest of them also raised their hands and David said, "I think we are all in."

"Whew," and Joe sighed, "that's a relief."

At lunch, Elise asked Joe, "Did you know that I spoke Spanish?"

He smiled sheepishly, "You know, I do think that I saw that on your resume' when I was interviewing the team. I'd forgotten it until you mentioned it though. I didn't realize how handy it was going to become. How fluently do you speak it?"

She looked down at the table, "Some of the foster homes I grew up in spoke it, but the first words I learned probably shouldn't be repeated in public."

Joe reached over and touched the back of her hand to get her attention. She looked up, "They might come in handy in the list of words not to add to the transcript of the Spanish text."

At least her lips smiled, "Probably."

They brought on two other native Spanish speakers to the team, Carlos, another systems analyst, and Juanita, another coder. The additions seemed to fit right in and they continued to grow together as a team. They worked hard together and apart. Mostly they just plain worked hard. Friday nights Joe took them all out to a local tavern. The food was on him, the alcohol on them. Actually, none of them drank very much, mostly because they would be back in on Saturday which wasn't conducive to a hangover. That, and they were just a really nice group of hard working folk.

As it drew near the Christmas break they had all but forgotten about the company dinner and the Tim-DOS award. As the old saying goes, "When you are knee-deep in alligators it is difficult to remember that the original plan was to drain the swamp." The Spanish version had come with its own set of incredible problems. To create the independent user version had been like having to teach an adult how to distinguish colored symbols. With the Spanish version it was like having to teach an infant to crawl, walk, then run.

Chapter Eighteen
The Tim-DOS Award

The Monday before the all-company Christmas dinner, invitations had shown up in every employee's inbox. Joe mentioned it at their morning meeting. "Don't forget, Thursday night is the all-company Christmas dinner. Bring your 'plus-one' and be dressed to the T's as we will be receiving special recognition." Joe looked at their latest additions to the team, Juanita and Carlos, and addressed them. "You have undoubtedly heard about our last project."

Carlos interrupted him, "Yup, that's why we were so eager to join you. We wanted to be on the winning team," and he snickered.

"Well, if you can keep a secret, and I'm sure that you can, we will be awarded the coveted Tim-DOS award at the dinner. So, while you can't join us for the award, you can bask in the light of now being on the winning team," and Joe laughed too.

Thursday arrived all too quickly. Joe got home early, conked on the couch for an hour, then took his shower and got ready. Elaine had taken the day off, so she was already ready when he came home. As he lay there on the couch she almost joined him, but then she would have had to get ready all over again. She let him sleep and when he was finally all dressed up, they traveled across town to the restaurant.

Each year, Dragoon would take over the entire upstairs of one of the town's swankiest restaurants for their company's Christmas dinner. Everything on the menu was available, although alcohol was kept to a minimum, initially. Joe sat with Elaine on his right and with Elise and the rest of his team and their plus ones on his left.

Finally, after a scrumptious dinner, JR stood up and stepped up to the podium to enthusiastic applause. "Thank you," and he raised his hand until the applause died down. He chuckled, "Besides your Christmas bonus, I hope this dinner is something you look forward to every year." There was more applause and even a few whistles. "This is also our opportunity to recognize one team for outstanding achievement by awarding them the Tim-DOS award. Without Tim and his application to allow CPM software to run on the DOS operating system we would have never gotten here," and JR pointed to the floor at his feet, "and without this team we would never have remained the number one speech recognition software in the industry. This year's Tim-DOS award goes to Joe Huddlestom and his IUSA team for making *'Plain Speaking'* user independent! Joe, bring your team up here."

They got up and stood to the right of JR and the podium: David, Joe, Elise, Ted, Carl, Nate, and Janice. JR attempted to hand the microphone to Joe, but he didn't take it. Instead, he took David and Elise's hands, as Elise took Ted's, and on down the line. Joe then spoke into the mic that JR still held, "To the best team I have ever had the privilege to work with," and he looked up and down the line, "Thank you!" He raised David and Elise's hands to the thunderous applause of the entire company still seated at their tables. If that wasn't enough, they all began to get up out of their seats to make it a standing ovation.

JR then reached back to the podium, picked up the plaque, and attempted to hand the Tim-DOS award to Joe, but he still held David and Elise's hands. Joe looked at David, who then took the plaque from JR, and raised it in his left hand as Joe raised his other hand and Elise's again. More thunderous applause lasted until JR raised his own hand again, "Thank you again, Joe, and your team," and he looked over the crowd. "Please make sure that every table has a 'designated driver' while you enjoy the rest of the evening."

On the drive home, Joe was surprised to find Elaine especially silent and even a little distant. He asked, "Is something wrong?"

"What's the name again of the gal who sat to your left tonight?" She spoke with a distinct edge to her words.

"You mean Elise, the junior coder on our team?" he responded.

"You know she has a crush on you, don't you?" she spoke, cutting each word short.

"Don't be silly, she just appreciates having been added to a team that was able to accomplish so much this year. She was a valuable addition to all we did. Without her unique ability to turn requirements into elegant code, we probably would still be working on the project. She saved our bacon more than once." Joe was almost offended at the suggestion.

Elaine only uttered a, "Hmmm," and nothing more all evening. When Joe came to bed she was already asleep as far away from him on the bed as she could possibly be.

Chapter Nineteen
Work, Work, Work

They spent the entire next year working on the Spanish version. It proved more difficult than they had anticipated. No Tim-DOS award this year, although his team's work was still stellar. They were finishing up the user interface and then it would be ready for initial testing. Maybe they would have something to show the leadership team by Valentine's day.

Elise had recently introduced Joe to the smooth jazz of Julie and Donald Page. There was something classic about it and something softly melancholy. Even the improvs did not seemed to detract from the beauty of it like some modern improvs would. Everything about it seemed to resonate with him, deeply. Elise brought him a thumb drive of the songs she had which he loaded onto his phone and practically devoured. He wondered why he didn't share any of them with Elaine. It was like they were too personal. He needed something to be just for himself, like his relationship with Elise. That should have been a red flag too, but Joe wasn't particularly looking for any red flags.

Elise and Joe's relationship continued to grow. Elise walked into the lunch room where Joe already sat at a table, "Good morning, Joe."

He smiled, "Nearly afternoon. When was the last time I told you that you have the uncanny ability of being able to take the customer's requirements and turn them into the code that does exactly what was requested and does it extremely efficiently? I will have you on all my future teams, if it's up to me." He was running a copy of their latest Spanish version on his laptop.

She blushed, "You tell me often, but thank you, anyway." They had began to meet for working lunches, but some of the lunches were not as efficient at getting work done as they were about exploring their relationship. "Why do you suppose it is that we seem to work so well together?"

He stopped, his sandwich only halfway to his mouth, "I don't know that I have really thought about it, you?"

She giggled behind her napkin, "I think we were linked, joined in a prior lifetime."

He shook his head behind his sandwich, "Ah… that would explain it. Either that or you're Wiccan and have placed a spell on me." He put his sandwich down, "No, really?"

Elise widened her eyes, "You thought I was joking?" Then her eyes returned to normal, "I was. Actually, I think we just try harder when we are together than others do. They don't really care as much. I know that it's more than just a job for them, but we, on the other hand, do care, a lot. We not only think that what we do matters, but that it makes a difference, and so it does."

"So, motive and attitude, leading to better action?" he summarized.

"That might explain it. However, we could just be better than most," and she chuckled.

"Better, that too would explain it," and he joined her chuckle.

He finished the last bite of sandwich, grabbed his bottle of diet pop, and as he stood up, said, "Well, should we go be better than most with the rest of the team?" He extended his hand for a high-five which she gave him as she too rose from her chair.

Chapter Twenty
An Earlier Lunch

Joe remembered a few weeks earlier when they were having lunch. He had whispered a word. It sounded like "Urim," the name of the sacred stone of lights, but it had been more ancient than that.

Elise had responded as if he had just tipped over his coffee onto the table. "What?" she had visibly recoiled.

He had whispered it again as he looked into her eyes and he seemed to find a spark of recognition there. "Do you know the story about the Garden of Eden?"

"The fable of Adam and Eve?" she responded, her eyes now registering skepticism.

His eyes smiled in return, "Some would consider it more than a fable."

Her eyes softened a little, "Surely, no educated man?"

Joe looked down at the table, "Nevermind."

But she reached over and touched the back of his hand, next to the still full cup of coffee, "No, go ahead."

He took a slow deep breath, "It records there being two trees in the center of that Garden."

"Two trees?" she questioned. "I thought Eve ate the apple off the one tree that was there, the tree of the knowledge of good and evil?"

Joe snickered, "It wasn't an apple and there was another tree there," he said confidently.

"Well, you probably know the fable better than I," she conceded, "What was the other tree?"

Ah, it was his opening. "It was called the Tree of Life." There. He'd said it!

"And the other was the tree of death?" She was being facetious.

"Hmmm, interesting that you should ask that. The word used for 'knowledge' in the original language sounds a lot like our English word 'death.'"

"And the Tree of Life?" she countered.

He hesitated, waiting for direction, and felt he got it.

"Did you ever see 'Fiddler on the Roof'?" he ventured.

"I did, it's one of my favorites," she responded.

"Remember the tavern scene when the butcher is asking for the hand of Tevye's daughter in marriage?" She nodded. "After they have sealed the deal they all sing, "To life, to life, la chaim. La chaim, la chaim, to life…." She nodded again. "La Chaim is Hebrew or 'to life.' Chaim means 'life'. Actually it is plural, so it might be better translated, 'lives.' Or as I like to think of it: cha, cha, cha, chachacha, laughter. It wasn't that one tree was good and the other bad, but that they were so incredibly different."

She remarked with surprise, "You know quite a bit about a fable!"

He looked almost longingly into her eyes, "What if it was more than that? What if it was a reality so profound that it was difficult to describe?"

She spoke slowly still surprised, "You're kidding?"

He took a slow deep breath, "I couldn't be more serious."

All she could utter was, "Hmmm."

"It might be something worth contemplating," he almost pleaded. "What if the God of the universe desired to have a relationship with you? A personal relationship with you?"

She laughed lightly, "I think you are just having me on."

He held her eyes carefully, "Not in the slightest. I am completely serious." He reached out his hand, but she just looked at it. That was unusual, but he wasn't sure if it was good or bad. "If you'd read the first three chapters of Genesis I would be happy to answer any questions that you have."

She shook her head slightly, "And you want me to read it as though it recorded fact?"

He looked up and to his right, "Read it like it was a novel and we can start there."

That incited another, "Hmmm, I'll think about it," and they left it at that. She never brought it up again.

Chapter Twenty-One
Garage-ware

Late Thursday afternoon, Joe clandestinely asked Nate and Ted to stick around after the others left by sending them separate e-mails. Elise tried to stay late too, but he walked her to the elevator and wished her a good weekend. Joe went into the conference room and after waiting an extra ten minutes to make sure they were alone, Nate and Ted joined him at the table.

Joe handed each of them a sheet of paper entitled "Ghost Proposal." He began, "I would like you two to join me on an extracurricular activity. I want to develop an App that will turn a cell phone into a ghost." Even though it was the end of a long week that perked them both up. They looked at the proposal and both looked up from it at the same time.

Nate spoke first and that was unusual, "This looks interesting. Where will you host it?"

Joe responded quickly, "I'm assembling us an office in my garage. I have purchased a couple of Dragoon's surplus servers. That should get us started."

Ted jumped in next, "It's funny, I have been working on an App, but didn't know what it was for. It seemed sort of silly, but now makes a whole lot of sense."

Joe again, "So, are you guys in?" They both looked at each other and nodded. "We'll also need a coder. I was thinking Elise?"

Ted piped up again, "Not to sound chauvinistic, but if we are going to be spending a lot of time alone together in a garage, it might be advantageous to be an all male team."

Joe looked down at the table, "Good point. Do you think Carl would be interested in joining us?"

Nate answered for the both of them, "Yes, I'm pretty sure he would. Anything we could do with you would be our pleasure, even if it's extracurricular."

"Wonderful," exclaimed Joe, obviously pleased, "I'll give him a call when I get home. When would you like to start?"

Both men looked at each other and said nearly in chorus, "This Saturday?"

"Great!" Nate and Ted got up, took the proposals with them, gathered up their laptops, coats, and went home.

Thus began the birth of "Archer," the Ghost app. Nate developed the "Quiver," a database to store everything. Ted built the "Bow," a search engine that launched everything out into cyberspace without it being tracked on its way out or on its way back leveraging "Voice over Internet Protocol" VoIP and WiFi technology. Joe built the "Arrows," the widgets that invisibly accomplished specific tasks. Carl had joined them and turned everything into elegant code as fast as he could. They began to work most Saturdays, often a couple evenings during the week since Elaine worked nights. It seemed the project was coming along splendidly.

One afternoon, Elise caught Joe alone, "What are you and the boys, except David, doing? You often seem to be having little clandestine meetings and lunches. We haven't had a working lunch in ages. Are you mad at me?"

Joe sighed, "I'm sorry. You're right! I guess I have been a little preoccupied." He looked at his calendar, "Let's have lunch today."

She brightened up, "Okay."

At lunch they sat over in the corner away from most everyone. Joe took a moment of silence before Elise came over and sat down to give thanks. Then he picked up his sandwich. It reminded him of the old joke about the guy who complained each day as he opened his lunch, "Peanut Butter again!" Finally one day his coworker asked, "Why don't you have your wife make you something different? To which he responded, "My wife? I make my own lunches."

He waited until she got settled and then started with, "The secret is that me and the boys," and he winked, "are working a little side project in my garage."

She inquired, "Can I be of any assistance?"

Joe sighed, "I did think of you when we started, but the guys felt that if we were going to be working all hours in my garage that it might be a good idea if we were all guys."

She frowned, "That sounds sort of lame."

"Probably, but that's the way they felt." He paused, "We might need some help when we get to the beta test, if you'd like?"

Now it was her turn to sigh. "Ok, however I can help." The rest of lunch concerned their progress on the Spanish version.

They had all worked together again late, had dinner brought in and worked until they began to get silly. Joe finally expressed it for them all, "I think we all better go home before we write some sloppy, stinking code."

Carl responded, "Yeah, like you write code."

Janice mimicked his tone, "Maybe not, but his point is valid. Let's go home." They closed their laptops and struggled to their feet, grabbed their coats, and headed out the door.

Ted chimed in, "You don't need to tell me twice."

Elise held back until she and Joe were alone, "Remember, my car is in the shop. Could you drop me off at home?"

"Sure," and he put on his jacket then helped her with her coat.

Chapter Twenty-Two
Elise's Home

They parked in Elise's driveway. She had a nice little two bedroom house with an attached garage. Joe got out and went over to her side to open her door, but she already had it open. He at least stood by it as she got out and walked with her to her door. He stood there as she unlocked it, and opened it with a, "Do you want to come in for a minute? I just got a new album by the Page's and there's one song you've just got to hear."

He felt a little "check" in his spirit, but he dismissed it with the thought, *"Five minutes, how could that matter?"* He said, "Okay, but just for a minute."

She closed the door, turned, held out her hand and asked, "Coat?" He felt another "check," but shrugged off his coat as well.

She pointed to the couch, "Have a seat." He did so reluctantly. At least that is what he told himself. He sat back and tried to relax. She was back in a flash with two cups of coffee. She handed him his, set hers on the coffee table and walked to an old stereo console. She pressed a few buttons and some soft smooth classic jazz quietly filled the room.

Joe took a sip of his coffee, placed it on the table, sat back, and closed his eyes. He must have drifted off. He was startled awake when he felt a hand on his thigh. He opened his eyes to find Elise leaning towards him, obviously looking like she was going to kiss him. He jumped away from her and got quickly to his feet. He exclaimed, "I am really sorry. I think you have gotten the wrong impression." He stumbled towards the door, grabbing his coat on the way. He said again, "I'm sorry," opened the door and left. He stood by his car, breathing deeply of the night air.

He heard the door open behind him, "You're a monster, Joe Huddleston!" The door slammed. He got in the car and drove home.

He sat at the coffee table, drinking a cup of coffee. A cup of hot water sat on it for Elaine when she got home. He saw her lights as she drove into the driveway and opened the door as she approached it. He would have hugged her, but she reached out a hand, palm on his chest, and restrained him.

Dejectedly she said, "I lost a patient tonight, in my arms."

Joe sat on the couch and patted the place next to him, "I'm so sorry. Can we talk about it?"

Elaine shrugged, "I don't want to talk. I just want to go to bed." She walked towards the hall that led to the bathroom and bedrooms.

Joe sat and stewed for a minute. Then he got up, took the two cups, rinsed them, and put them in the dishwasher. He stood at the sink a few minutes, just looking out the kitchen window. Then he followed his wife to bed. She was asleep before he could even get in his pajamas, let alone into bed. He rolled away from her and tried to fall asleep, but couldn't. He got back up, put on his robe, and went to the kitchen. He composed a letter describing the entire fiasco of his own evening at Elise's house. He printed it to his printer in his office, put it on the kitchen table next to his laptop, and went to bed.

Chapter Twenty-Three
Not Just Another Day

When she finally dragged herself out of bed she felt a little better. Sleep had helped put some distance between her and the death of her patient. Mr. Duply had been doing so well and she would have almost considered him a friend. Then, "boom," he was gone. It was an sudden heart attack and he had a "Do not resuscitate" order on his chart. She was giving him his last medications for the evening and holding his hand to say "good night," when it hit him. He looked up at her with shock and pain in his eyes as he clutched his chest. Then his eyes softened, he smiled, and was gone. She hadn't even had time to take his pulse, just hold his hand and look him in the eyes sympathetically.

In her bathroom, she splashed some water on her face, dried off, and walked to the kitchen for some hot water. That's when she saw the letter. She read it as her water heated up. She was shocked, but not surprised. She had warned him.

His laptop sat open on the kitchen table when her phone pinged, a text message. It was from an unrecognized phone number, "Check his laptop!" "*What?*" she thought. She hit the spacebar and the screen saver came up asking for his password. She knew it, so she entered it. His email account was displayed, open to an email from Elise, and a photo of her in bed, undressed, and posed in a provocative manner. She quickly closed the email only to have it be replaced by one from a week earlier, of Elise in her bedroom, taken from the back, in panties, and a bra she was unclasping. She closed it, to be replaced by another. She slammed the laptop closed. She thought, "He says he got up and left. Do I believe him? Then what about all these emails and photos?" She didn't even pour her hot water. She got up and took a shower.

She sat at her dressing table, looking into the mirror. "*Am I that ugly?*" she thought. "*Have I changed that much?*" She put on her makeup on autopilot, then made the bed, and began packing for her trip. In the middle of packing, she was thinking of how a week away might add some perspective. Then she had an additional thought, "*Am I coming back? This betrayal is too deep. Adultery is grounds for divorce.*" At the conference, if she put herself 'out there' she could probably have another job in another city before she returned home. "*Hmmm.*" She packed a second bag and all her toiletries.

The guys did not come over on that Saturday, so he just sat round, watched football, and had a pizza. The afternoon on Sunday was much the same, except he added ice cream, his go to comfort food. He called Elaine a number of times, but only got her voicemail. He left the same message each time: "Missing you, call me." About the fourth time it probably started sounding rote. Sunday night, he went to bed early.

Elise had not come to work last Friday or that next Monday. He was a bit disappointed. "*Should I call her?*" He didn't. When Joe got to the office on Tuesday, he found a note on his work laptop, "JR wants to see you, 9:00am in his office." "*Hmmm,*" he wondered if they were close enough on completing the Spanish version that JR was preparing him for the next project. When he got to the office, he saw Anita from HR was also in attendance.

Joe entered and acknowledged them, "JR, Anita."

Anita addressed him, "Have a seat, Joe," and she pointed to the other side of the table in JR's office. He sat on that side and they sat on the other. Anita slid a sheet of paper across the desk to Joe. He looked at it and was shocked. It showed Elise on a bed in a rather compromising position. Joe quickly turned it over, face down, on the desk as Anita asked, "Do you recognize her?"

"Of course I do. That's Elise, she works for me," he could barely get the words out.

"Yesterday, she filed a sexual harassment case against you and that is one of the photos found in emails between the two of you." Anita continued, concern covering her face and lacing her words.

"You've got to be kidding. There must be some mistake!" Joe was shocked.

"No, there can be no mistake. There were over a dozen emails over the last two months, many of them with photos similar to this one. We are putting you on administrative leave immediately, pending the results of our investigation." Anita spoke calmly and directly.

JR added, "Joe, you know we have a zero tolerance policy towards this kind of thing. Security is outside the door. Please leave the building immediately and we'll let you know our decision after we have completed the review."

"Can I talk to her?" he nearly whimpered.

Anita answered again, "That would not be a good idea. There must be absolutely no contact between you and her until this is cleared up."

Security walked him to his desk. The team looked at him questioningly, but he just shrugged, picked up his stuff, and left. In the car he disregarded Anita's advice and called Elise. "This phone has been disconnected," was the only answer he received. He sat there for a few minutes with his head in his hands. Then he drove home. At home he called Elaine. She was probably in meetings so he expected to only get her voice mail. What he heard shocked him even more, "This phone has been disconnected." *"What, hers too? Is this some kind of conspiracy?"* He hadn't used his home laptop since he'd typed up the note for Elaine. He opened his laptop to send her an email and found his email already opened. He was staring at another provocative photo of Elise. He looked far too long. That's when the realization finally hit him square in the face. While he hadn't committed physical adultery with Elise, he had been guilty of an emotional affair. He had given to her his time, attention, and affections that by rights belonged only to his wife. He slammed the lid down on his laptop, lay down on the couch as the guilt washed over him. Emotionally exhausted he finally fell asleep.

He opened his eyes. The doorbell rang incessantly. At the door he found a Western Union delivery man, "You have a telegram." Joe tipped him and he left. "Who sends telegrams nowadays?" He opened it. It was from Elaine.

"I have seen the photos STOP You will be hearing from my lawyer STOP All I want is my car and half the value of the house STOP Do not try and contact me STOP"

He fell to his knees and then to the floor, "No!" He screamed.

On Friday, he received a phone call from HR at Dragoon. It was Anita, "Joe, I'm sorry. After conducting our investigation it has been determined that the evidence is conclusive. You have been terminated and a severance check is in the mail."

"But I have not been called as a witness in the inquiry. Do I not get a chance to speak my piece?" Joe pleaded.

Anita repeated herself, "I'm sorry, nothing you could say would make any difference. The weight of the evidence left us no recourse, but to terminate you. Again, I'm sorry," and she hung up. Joe sat on the couch, and wept.

That Saturday the guys came and knocked at the door of the house when there was no answer at the garage. Joe opened the door reluctantly. He looked like he hadn't slept well in days. They followed him into the kitchen where they all sat at the kitchen table. Joe asked without much enthusiasm, "Would you guys like a cup of coffee?"

Ted got up. "I'll get it." He filled a teapot for the hot water and Joe slumped back down to the table. "What's going on Joe? Elise left, you've left, they're telling us nothing."

Joe looked long at his friends before he spoke. “Elise accused me of sexual harassment. Some compromising photos of her showed up on my computer. They have decided to believe her and have terminated me.” He put his head in his hands. He wanted to cry again.

Ted was spooning dried coffee into their cups. “So, what’s the real story?”

Joe took a deep breath, “As well as I can piece it together?” He took another deep breath. “After we we received the Tim-DOS award, my wife told me Elise had a crush on me. I put it off to female jealousy. But in hindsight, I should have believed her. On Thursday night last week, when I dropped her off at her home since her car was in the shop, she asked me in to hear a new song from a group we both like. I sat on her couch, listening to some music. I closed my eyes for a minute, I might have dozed off, but I awakened to find her hand on my thigh and I think she was leaning in to kiss me.” He took a long drink of coffee. “I jumped up, told her she was mistaken, and left. I think she must have been really mad and very hurt.” He took another drink, “While this next part is speculation, I think she decided to hurt me back, took a bunch of compromising photos of herself, and then hacked my home and work computers.”

Carl joined in, “That’s entirely possible, she is that good. She once confided to me that early in her college career she had done some hacking just for fun, and never got caught.”

Ted spoke again, “So, what are you going to do?”

Resigned, Joe answered, “There is nothing I can do. She totally convinced them and they won’t give me a hearing. To make matters worse, my wife found the photos on my home computer, and has chosen to believe them too. She’s left me.”

Carl looked shocked, “You’re kidding.”

Joe shook his head, “I wish I was.”

Ted interjected, “Do you want us to go to bat for you?”

Carl added, “Yeah, do you?”

Nate finally added his two-cents, "You know, looking back, I think there were signs that she became infatuated with you. I thought it was just her appreciation for making her a part our team."

Joe slipped in his, "Me too."

Nate finished his thought, "but in retrospect, sorry mate."

"Well, I don't want you guys getting involved," and Joe looked at each of them. "I don't want the stink of it getting on any of you."

"So, what do we do?" Carl looked searchingly at Joe.

Joe smiled weakly, "I guess at least I'll be able to work full time on the Archer App."

Ted scrambled to his feet. "Fill up your cups and let's go do it!

Chapter Twenty-Four
Sabbath's End

The letter from Elaine's lawyer came in the morning mail. It said, "Do not try to contact her. She has a restraining order against you. Please sign this document, sign the letter releasing the title of her car to her, and include a check for half the fair market value of the house." He placed the letter on his Bible and cried. His grief could not have been more if she had died. She had died, at least to him. When he had finished, he dried his eyes and looked at the rest of the mail.

Also in the post was a severance check from Dragoon. It was for a very large sum. It also included a travel voucher for his part of the "Tim-DOS" award for him and a plus one. He could cash in the voucher, probably sell off about one third of his Dragoon stock, and make up the difference in the half of the house's value that he owed Elaine. He called his broker. He was fortunate that the stock was at an all time high, a good time to sell. By the end of the week he had the check written, the documents signed, and included a note asking where he should send the rest of her clothes and personal items which he had boxed up.

Joe snuck into the basement at the back of the room and sat down. He was ashamed that he had been skipping Sabbath service because of the work they were doing in the garage. He knew the Archer App was important, but it was not *'that'* important. He realized that he had lost touch with an essential part of himself, a part of life itself. There seemed to be so much loss at the present. He spent most of the entire worship service looking at his feet. He never got up to dance.

Rabbi Shammah stood, "Joe, come up here."

Joe's head snapped up like a prairie dog looking out of his hole. He had thought himself unseen. He was mistaken. He thought of bolting out the back, escaping, but instead slowly stood. He walked up to the front of the room and stood next to his Rabbi, his head still down.

Rabbi reached out and lifted Joe's chin, "When Rabbi Jesus was dealing with the woman taken in adultery, at nearly the end of that passage that many do not think even belongs in the gospel of John, He says to her, 'Neither do I condemn you, go and sin no more.' And I say to you Joe, 'Neither do I condemn you, go and sin no more.'" Joe began to sob and Rabbi Shammah embraced him until the sobbing finished. He whispered in his ear, "You may return to your seat." He then began to speak on unconditional love that required unconditional forgiveness and included the "seventy times seven" passage that Jesus had spoken to Peter. His words were like honey, but Joe didn't really hear any of them. He just sat there, his head in his hands, basking in the forgiveness he had been granted. While he sat there, one person after another walked up to him and laid their hands on him. They didn't say anything, just touched him for a minute. It was powerful beyond explanation and he basked in that too. He wanted to weep, but he was having a hard enough time to just keep his breathing even. The chorus to the song "More than Wonderful" played through his heart and mind:

For He's more wonderful than my mind can conceive
He's more wonderful than my heart can believe
He goes beyond my highest hopes and fondest dreams
He's everything that my soul ever longed for
Everything He's promised and so much more
More than amazing, more than marvelous

More than miraculous could ever be
He's more than wonderful, that's what Jesus is to me.

The next thing he knew he was sitting all by himself. The others had left. He slowly got up from his chair, took a deep breath, left the building, and walked home. It definitely felt like the end of an era and the start of a new chapter.

Chapter Twenty-Five
After the Conference

The nursing conference had been amazing. If she hadn't been dealing with Joe's betrayal she would have had a lot of fun. At least much of it was distracting from her current predicament. She had also gotten the ball rolling. She got a new phone, got in touch with a lawyer and the divorce papers would be served citing his infidelity as the cause. All she wanted was her car and to be paid off for her half of the house. She had already cancelled her bank accounts and reopened them in a different bank. She even got some perks for that. She let it be known that she was looking for a job and her reputation had already resulted in three offers. She was leaning towards a small hospital in rural Indiana, Ascension St. Vincent. She talked with their HR, they emailed her the paperwork, and a recommendation of a realtor.

Elaine had half a dozen homes to look at via their listings by the following day. She signed the paperwork, changed her ticket to Indianapolis and a puddle-jumper to North Vernon Municipal. Joe had signed off the title to her car and she had a cash offer the next day. It was almost scary how fast everything worked to her benefit. She had two weeks vacation that she took from her old job and used it as her two weeks notice. They weren't tickled, but she had them over a barrel. They gave her glowing references regardless, as she had been a stellar employee until her husband's affair.

She had even had a couple of nice dinners with some male nurses during the conference who heard she was separated from and divorcing her husband. Wow! Word traveled fast. She wasn't looking for anything romantic, but at least it was good for her morale. By the end of the conference she was heading towards a whole new life.

North Vernon turned out to be all she could have possibly hoped for. Ascension gave her a week to get settled and for them to figure out exactly where they wanted her. She asked if it were possible to start on second shift and they fell all over that possibility. To have someone of her caliber on second shift thrilled them to no end. She found a small bungalow a block off the local transit line and she was able to make a large down payment with her savings. Once Joe paid off his half of her old house, she could pay the house off in full with plenty to spare. The bungalow came partially furnished and she didn't need much else. A little thrift store shopping, some towels and bedding from the local Big Mart and she was set. She even found a decent flat screen TV from a local secondhand computer shop for a very deep discount.

Through her lawyer she had been able to change her name back to her grandmother's maiden name and she was pretty sure that Joe had no idea what it was. Everything was purchased in her new name. Except through her lawyer, she was virtually untraceable. Slowly she began to rebuild her life. The Hebrew word normally used for peace is Shalom, but there is another word similar to the word for justice called Meshar. Joe had taught her an ancient version of it and, regardless of her feelings for Joe, she whispered softly each night before she went to bed and each morning when she first awoke and it became the foundation of her new life. It was a different kind of peace.

North Vernon did not have a large Jewish population, but there were enough men for a synagogue. She began attending it each Sabbath, once she had worked second shift long enough to be granted Friday and Saturdays off. She thrived at the hospital, partly because she carried the peace with her. It was nearly palatable. She took all the hard patients and they became putty in her hands. Soon, Ascension wondered how they had ever gotten along without her. They didn't know about her husband's supposed unfaithfulness or they would have blessed the day it had brought her to them.

Chapter Twenty-Six
A New Chapter

How do you start a new chapter? One word at a time. Initially Joe had packed up just the rest of Elaine's clothes and toiletries, but decided to add the household things that he would never use. He went through the kitchen and boxed up most of the plates, pans, etc. that he wouldn't need. He did the same with most all of the cupboards and storage areas in the house. He had received a letter by return mail from her lawyer stating that a friend of Elaine's, Jacob, would stop by on Friday with a truck to haul her things away. Well, that would save him a lot of UPS postage. Jacob shook Joe's hand, introduced himself as Elaine's friend, and seemed a nice enough guy. He was a little surprised at how many boxes there were, but had an empty panel van so it didn't really matter. Joe helped him load and then said goodbye to all of Elaine's stuff and his final fleeting contact with her. He did ask Jacob to wish Elaine well for him. He said he would.

Monday morning Joe found himself at Chick-fil-A. He had passed by it often enough, even knew of their trademarked, "My pleasure," but had never eaten there. Perhaps this was part of his new chapter. He ordered a chicken, egg, and cheese muffin, hash browns, and a cup of coffee (3 cream & 3 sugars). He went and sat at a table just outside the enclosed kids play area. There was no one else in the dining room except a couple of guys who had nodded to him as he passed by on his way to the table he had chosen.

A young gal, her name tag said Julie, brought him his food and pointed to a sticker on the table. "If you point your phone's camera at the QR code," and she pointed to it, "and then press the link that appears, you can download our app, earn points, and next time order right from your table."

He thanked her and was not disappointed as she responded with, "My pleasure." Her genuine smile seemed to prove that she really meant it. She additionally asked if he needed any sauces.

"What do you have?" he replied.

"Lots! Ranch, Polynesian, barbecue, our own Chick-fil-A sauce which is like a honey mustard…." She waited.

Joe sighed, "Ranch, please."

She nodded at the two gentlemen seated just around the corner from the counter as she passed and returned promptly with two ranch sauce containers. Opening them was a challenge. They were obviously child-proof, almost adult-proof too, but he finally got it open and without spilling any. He opened the hash browns to find out that they were like tater-tots. When dipped in the ranch sauce they were quite good. They were gone almost before he knew it. He opened the foil-wrapped muffin. It was still warm and extremely good. He had just folded up the wrapper to the muffin and placed it and the empty sauce container in the hash brown box, when an older athletic gentleman, stepped up to his table and extended a hand.

"Jeremy," he said, "May I join you?"

"Ah… sure," and Joe shook his hand, "Joe."

"I haven't seen you in here before," Jeremy stated as he sat down.

"Nope, first time. I've driven by a lot, but never stopped in until this morning." Joe was surprised how easy it was to talk to him.

"And what do you think?" Jeremy gestured around the place.

"Ah, I like it. Nice atmosphere, quiet, good food," Joe admitted.

"Breakfast is the best time. Lunch and dinner times can be a bit chaotic," Jeremy stated matter-of-factly.

Joe chuckled, "I'll try to remember that."

"It's still a great place even then, just not as quiet and calming as it is now. So, to ask a 'guy question,' what do you do?"

Joe thought about how he should respond. "I'm working freelance on a software development project."

Jeremy probed deeper, "And your target market is?"

Joe smiled shyly and looked down at the table, "I can't say too much about it. It's sort of a secret."

Jeremy smiled himself, "Oh, it's for the government?"

Joe looked sideways to the right and then to the left as he whispered, "Actually it is sort of 'anti-government,' rather for the people."

Jeremy whispered back, "Interesting, and it will help the people how?"

Joe shook his head, "Sorry, I've probably said too much already. What do you do?"

Jeremy took a deep breath, "A little bit of this, a little bit of that."

Joe scrunched his eyebrows, "That's a little vague isn't it?"

Jeremy chuckled, "Sorry. Let's see," he appeared to think a moment, "my last assignment involved a kitten stuck in a tree."

"Oh, you're a fireman," Joe responded.

"*Hmmm*," Jeremy mused, "A hook and ladder truck would have been convenient. Unfortunately, I had to climb the tree free-hand."

Joe was surprised. "And come back down holding a kitten in one hand?"

Jeremy chuckled, "Fortunately, she fit in my shirt, and better yet didn't scratch me."

"I'll bet some kid was happy!" Joe exclaimed.

Jeremy stopped chuckling reluctantly, "Yes, as was the girl's mother." Out of the blue Jeremy asked, "Are you a Christian?"

Surprised again, Joe asked, "Where did that come from?"

"It's just a question. Are you?" Jeremy pushed lightly.

Joe looked at him a little askance. "That term has too many bad connotations now days. I would say that I am a follower of Jesus."

Jeremy pushed a little more, "Do you study the Scriptures?"

This question was simpler. "I do."

"Would you like to meet here and do it together?" Jeremy asked, this time without a push.

Joe cocked his head a little to the right as he answered, "I would actually."

"A friend of mine wrote what he affectionately calls 'The Gospel According to Nick.' It includes a twenty-seven week daily devotional. How about we try that?"

"You have a friend who translated one of the gospels?" Joe was curious now.

"He wrote it as a novel, but it is based on Scripture. It will provide a fresh and new perspective. I think you will like it." Jeremy seemed comfortable with it.

"Sure, I'm game if you are. Have you already read it?"

"I have, that's why I can say that I think you will like it." He reached down to the satchel that lay at his feet and removed a book from it. He placed it reverently on the table as he said, "It's only two chapters a week and some questions," and they went on to talk of other things.

Chapter Twenty-Seven
A New Day

Although it had been nearly three hundred pages in length, Joe had finished "Nate's Gospel" in one sitting. He had found it captivating, mesmerizing, and wholly transporting. It was like he was seeing everything for the first time, new and afresh. The daily devotional part was pretty easy, two chapters each week and a few questions. He reread the prologue and the first chapter.

Jeremy was already seated and eating when Joe arrived. He joined him at the table, they shook hands, and Joe submitted his order on the app. Between mouthfuls, Jeremy spoke, "So, what did you think?"

Joe folded his hands on the table, "Your friend wrote that?" Jeremy nodded. "Wow, I'll have you know I read the whole thing yesterday and reviewed the prologue and first chapter this morning. It is quite amazing."

After finishing his current chicken nugget, Jeremy added, "To look at my friend you wouldn't believe he was an 'internationally acclaimed' author either."

Julie brought Joe his breakfast for which he thanked her. Of course he got a, "My pleasure," in return. He removed his hat as he gave thanks for the day, for his expected time with Jeremy, and for his breakfast.

"Nick's prior book chronicled the travels of the Magi to find Jesus. It was a lot to recap in just a prologue," Jeremy explained.

"It does make me want to read that one too," Joe confessed. "So, did you answer the first question of the devotional?"

Jeremy placed a five-by-eight inch notebook on the table, "Yes, but I have problems writing in the actual book, a hold over from my education. I had Nate send me a PDF copy I could format to fit in my notebook. Would you like a copy to use yourself?"

Joe nodded, "That would be really nice. I have the same aversion to writing in books." He turned in his copy of the book to the question and read it out loud: "Why would five special people make the long and arduous journey to find the Promised One?" They talked about that and the followup question, "Why is that important to you?" for the next twenty minutes.

When they were through, Jeremy asked him, "Anything else?"

Joe took a deep breath, might have even gulped. "My wife left me." Jeremy nodded for him to go on and he did. He explained about the affair that his wife thought he had, but that he hadn't physically had and about the photo's that the woman had placed on his computer. They were pictures of her in compromising positions that he had never seen before. Similar pictures showed up at work along with an accusation of sexual harassment. He had been let go. He currently lived off his investments.

Jeremy asked him if he'd be interested in attending a seminar called, "Recovering from an Affair," even though he hadn't really had a physical one. He said that he'd think and pray about it. Jeremy smiled, "I know the presenter."

Joe laughed, "Do you know everyone?"

Jeremy laughed too, "Everyone, no, a lot of people, yes."

Right there Joe decided that he would call Jeremy's friend, "Can I have his number?"

The guys met Joe in the garage after work. They brought take out with them from the Chinese restaurant down the street. Joe asked them, "Why are we making this app?"

Carl smiled, "You've been reading 'Know Your Why' again, haven't you?"

Joe snickered, "No, it's just good to review our 'Why?' every once in a while."

Carl continued, "and this is that while?"

"Yeah, I guess."

"Well," Nate began, "with the way things are going, it may soon be a real advantage to be able to fly under the radar, so to speak."

Joe asked, "Are we planning to publish this to the planet?"

Carl jumped back in, "That would be sort of self-defeating wouldn't it? We would probably want to clandestinely publish a clandestine app, don't you think?"

Joe sighed, "Good, just checking."

Nate checked in again, "I think we should start rounding up some folks for the Beta test. We should be ready pretty soon."

Ted added, "I have a friend, who will remain anonymous, who is quite a hacker. I'm pretty sure he can hack into the system that is able to track all phone calls in the area. It would be able to demonstrate if the app is really working."

Joe laughed lightly, "So, should we target next Saturday?" They both nodded their agreement. "I'll get us half a dozen burner phones to work with, okay?"

Chapter Twenty-Eight
Beginning That Friday

They had met each morning at Chick-fil-A and gone over the morning devotional questions from "The Gospel According to Nick." Joe enjoyed reading it as much the second time as he had the first and the questions were helping him to go even deeper. Today's question "Why was the story of Mishimar's sword, Hane, important to the children?" was no exception.

Joe had responded, "Mystery and magic are always important to children. I wonder why we lose that growing up?"

To which Jeremy had said, "I don't think we have to. Didn't you say that you were a 'wind whisperer?' Isn't that a part of the mystery for you personally?"

Joe had almost forgotten that he had mentioned that in their discussion earlier that week. "Yes, I guess it is. Everything that surrounds Chayeem contains the fragrance of mystery and it is wonderful." They had basked in that wonder for a moment before Joe added, "I called Steve Schlesinger and he has agreed to meet with me next week after his seminar is completed."

"Good!" Jeremy sighed, "I think you will both like him and find him helpful."

Joe chuckled, "If you say so, that's good enough for me. Should we do the questions for weeks five, six, and seven for tomorrow and get caught up on doing "two chapters per day" rather than per week?"

Jeremy nodded, "Good idea." They chatted a bit more, prayed, and parted for the day.

The guys arrived to find printed copies of the documentation for the Archer app sitting on the desks where they normally sat. "I think everything is ready for our big day tomorrow. Ted, will your guy be joining us?"

Ted nodded, "Yes, but for him to remain anonymous he will be wearing a mask and we will not refer to him by name."

They each nodded as Ted looked at Joe, who said, "And we will each bring someone unknown to each other to perform the Beta test?" He received a chorus of agreement. "Assuming our success, I would like to take you guys out to dinner tomorrow night."

Ted piped up, "What, no trip to Tahiti?"

Joe laughed, "Nope, that's not within the budget. Okay, I'll see you tomorrow at my house at about ten in the morning."

Carl, Ted, and Joe each showed up with their guest in tow. Ted's anonymous friend, the hacker, had arrived early, in a mask, and was already in the garage getting inside the phone tracking system, preparing for the demonstration. Joe handed out the six burner phones and non-disclosure agreements for them all to sign, which they did. The phones were numbered one to six. Three of them were given the number of a phone to call. Phone number one called two, three called four, and five called six. They had walked out to the garage while the odd three dialed the even three on their burner phones to show that the phones were active and tracking in the system.

Joe and the rest of them gathered around the Hacker. "This is Frank," Joe snickered, "not his real name."

Masked Frank nodded, "I have all six phones active and accounted for by the national tracking system," and he pointed to his screen.

Joe instructed, "Press the Home key," and they all did. "Now, press the Archer icon."

They did that too, and all of them witnessed the phones disappear from Frank's screen, "Holy Toledo! It worked! They're all gone."

"Now, odd phones send a text to the evens," Joe requested. Lots of thumbs and forefingers typed. Each of the evens responded that they got the texts, "Got it. Yup, me too. Yup, I got one."

Frank responded, "Hmmm, no activity seen on my end."

Joe directed again, "Send a text back, evens." Still nothing on the screen. "Now, each of you search for something on the web."

More typing echoed in the garage, "I'm on Amazon. I'm looking at a YouTube video. I found a location on Google Maps."

Frank commented, "Still no activity showing up here."

Ted asked the friend he had brought, "Call me on my own cell phone." Ted's cell vibrated in his pocket and he answered it.

Frank spoke, "I've got Ted's phone showing, but still not the ghost cell."`

Joe smiled, deeply satisfied, "Anything else we should try?"

Carl spoke up, "Pay a bill."

"Good idea," Joe responded. "Can you pay your phone bill from your phone?" Carl nodded that he could. "Good, try it," Joe instructed.

"Okay, I'm on the phone company's website," Carl beamed.

"Still no activity," said Frank.

"Oops," Carl interjected, "They're sending a code to my cell phone." His cell in his pocket pinged, he took it out, and checked the code. He entered the code into the burner, accessed his account, and paid the bill.

He turned to Frank, "Did the phone company at any time appear to recognize the burner ghost phone?"

"Nope, not that I could see."

Someone suggested, "How about 911?"

"Naw, let's not push our luck there," Joe frowned. "Well, thanks for a successful Beta test. You can keep the burner phones as my gift to you. They are activated for a month. You can also keep the Archer app that is on them, but I ask that you not copy or clone it. Okay?" They all nodded. They all shook hands and the three friends left. Joe handed Frank a prepaid VISA card, "And most of all, thank you." Joe also handed him a burner phone. "When you have some time, please see if you can hack into our app and let Ted know of the result."

Frank's voice betrayed that he must be grinning mischievously. "I would love to, but with Carl on your team I'm pretty sure that I won't be able to break into it."

Carl was a little shocked, "You know me?"

Frank still sounded as though he was grinning, "Let's say, by reputation."

Carl raised his eyebrows. Frank shook Joe's hand and then he too departed.

It was Nate's turn, "After all that blood, sweat, and tears, it is still amazing that it really works."

Joe shook his head slightly, "I had every confidence that it would," and chuckled. "Let's sit down and debrief." When they were done, Joe added, "Back here for dinner at six?" They all nodded, shook hands again and left Joe in his garage. He sat there for a few minutes. "*Wow, that was unbelievable, even better than a Spanish version of the* 'Plain Speaking' *software.*" He sat there for a while longer, grateful for what they had accomplished. Too bad no one would ever know.

Chapter Twenty-Nine
Another Sabbath Service

Joe entered Sabbath service a little late. He sat in back again, but this time he participated in the singing and the dancing. When Rabbi Shammah sat down, so did everyone else. He prayed, stood up again, and faced his people, "Joe, could you come up here?" A bit hesitant, Joe complied. The Rabbi put his arm around Joe's shoulder and announced, "I think that you have a word for us today." He stepped away from Joe, turned, and sat back down.

Joe said something under his breath, probably, *"Help!"* Then he began, "Paul says in Second Corinthians chapter ten:

> The weapons of our warfare are not like the world's weapons, but are divinely powerful to the destruction of strongholds, destroying arguments and every lofty opinion raised against the knowledge of God, and to the taking every thought captive to obey Christ.

Firstly, I would point out that he says 'weapons.' There is often more than just one of them, maybe more than one of them for each of us. So, what are your weapons? Well, they are not guns, knives, or bombs. Those are the world's weapons. They are not even your arguments used to destroy their arguments. What will destroy their argument of 'God no longer heals miraculously?' Their child was just hit by a car and lies bleeding in the road. A young woman passing by, steps into the road, kneels down next to their daughter, and heals her. I think their argument just evaporated like the morning mist. What about their lofty opinion that is against the knowledge of God? Where they say, God is irrelevant. They're sitting on a park bench and a young man sits next to them. He asks to pray for them? They're so shocked that they can't even decline. He begins and suddenly it is like he has just been given a window into their soul. He asks God for aid in every area of their desperate need. Where is their lofty opinion now? I want us to take a moment and ask Him, 'What is my primary weapon,' and expect Him to share it with you. When He does, I would like you to stand."

It began as a moment of profound silence and then one person stood, then another, then another, until there were about twenty individuals standing.

Joe pointed to one gal, "Your weapon?"

She looked at the floor, "Kindness."

Joe responded, "Yes! It is the kindness of God that leads to…" and he paused.

His pause was filled in with a chorus of folks finishing the sentence, "…repentance."

Joe pointed to a middle-aged man, who said, "I have never thought of 'peace' as a weapon, but He said, 'Peace.'"

Joe again responded, "Yes! Whatever house you enter, first say, 'Peace be to this house,' and if a son of peace is there, your peace will rest upon him. Your 'peace' can change the environment, the atmosphere. It can make a difference in all that you do. Recognize it, use it…. strategically."

They went on for another ten minutes, with Joe pointing, and people sharing their weapons for the benefit of others to hear.

Rabbi Shammah finally stood, "Could we all stand for a closing prayer?" The rest of them joined the others who were still standing. "Thank you for a new understanding of the weapons You have placed in our hand. Lead us in this battle of light versus darkness, to make a difference everywhere we go this week."

There was a chorus of "Amen's."

Chapter Thirty
The Recovery Specialist

Steve Schlesinger specialized in Recovery, especially from the carnage of a broken relationship caused by one of the spouse's unfaithfulness. He had authored the book, "Affair-Proofing Your Marriage," that had become a run-away best-seller. He was rather expensive as a personal counselor, usually sharing in large group seminars instead, but as a special favor to their mutual friend Jeremy, he agreed to see Joe.

Joe sat in Steve's waiting room for a half an hour before the receptionist called his name and escorted him to Steve's door. Joe initially wondered where the prior appointment had gone. No one had come out the door. Seeing his consternation the receptionist said, "There's a separate exit for people when they are done seeing Dr. Schlesinger."

They introduced themselves and sat facing each other. Steve started, "How long have you known our friend Jeremy?"

"Not long," Joe replied, "but if you are as easy to talk to as he is, this should be a breeze."

Steve smiled, "Let's hope so. Tell me your story."

Joe sighed, "How long have I got?"

Steve still smiled, "As long as you need. I cleared my calendar for you."

Joe gulped, "Okay, here goes," and he told him the story as factually as he could. He did have to stop a few times and regain his composure.

Steve exclaimed slowly, "Wow, it sounds like you ended up with the wrong end of the stick."

Joe added, "and I feel like I was beaten with it."

"Jeremy tells me you are a follower of Jesus," Joe nodded, "and a wind whisperer?"

Startled, Joe said, "I guess I didn't tell Jeremy that was shared in confidence and he thought you should know."

Steve chuckled softly, "He's pretty perceptive, our Jeremy. I assume that you have forgiven all of them," Joe nodded. Steve dug a little deeper, "from the heart?"

Joe looked up quickly, "I'm not even sure I know what that means."

Steve coached gently, "To put it simply, it has to be more than just saying the words. Close your eyes." Joe did. "Picture yourself reading the telegram your wife left you." Joe began to sob. "Jesus is there, you may not see Him, but He is. Look around and find Him." Joe let out a big sob. "Where is He?

Joe whimpered, "Standing next to me with His arm around me."

Steve continued softly, "Ah….Feel His caring and compassion, let it soak in." Joe did for a few minutes. "Now how do you feel?"

Joe took a deep breath, "Strangely better, almost at peace."

Steve went on, "Remember when Jesus said to those who were crucifying Him, 'Father, I forgive them. They don't know what they are doing.' Your wife was doing what she felt she had to do. She wasn't trying to hurt you. So, now forgive her."

Joe began slowly, "Jesus, I forgive Elaine for leaving me." He was surprised how easily the words came out. The sting was mostly gone.

Steve spoke again, "Next, picture yourself looking at your computer, the one that now contains pictures of Elise. Now, this is a significant question," and he paused, "What was she feeling when she posted them?"

Joe saw himself sitting at the kitchen table, Jesus was sitting next to him with his hand covering the picture on the screen. Jesus was weeping. Joe had never seen Jesus weep before. He realized that Jesus was weeping at the hurt Elise had felt, hurt so deep that it had motivated her attack on him. Joe looked down at the table as the tears formed in his own eyes. He had told her that he was sorry that she had misunderstood their friendship. Now he was also sorry for the deep pain that he had caused her. He asked Jesus to forgive him and then whispered, "Elise, I am so sorry. I forgive you for acting out of the wound that I caused." Again, the sting was nearly gone.

Steve took a deep breath, "One more, your boss."

Joe took his own deep breath as he closed his eyes again. So much confusion, misunderstanding, and panicked action. The pink slip wasn't even pink. Jesus reached out and Joe handed him the not-pink slip. Jesus folded it up and put it in the sleeve of his robe. Joe took another deep breath, not as ragged this time, "JR, I forgive you. Anita, I forgive you and HR, and all those who believed the lies. I forgive them for thinking that I could possibly commit physical adultery against my wife. Jesus, forgive me for the emotional adultery that I did commit. I should have heeded the red flags and my wife's warning."

Joe looked up into Steve's face as Steve made the sign of the cross before his eyes. He said slowly "And I release you from the pain of all this." It was a declaration that reverberated in the air before him and then settled slowly into the depths of his heart. Another tear formed in the corner of Joe's eye as he mouthed, "Thank you."

Chapter Thirty-One
Back at Chick-fil-A

Joe and Jeremy sat at their regular seats at Chick-fil-A, going over the devotional, when a little boy walked up. Wait a minute, he wasn't a little boy, he was a young dwarf.

Jeremy reached out his hand to encompass the little hand that the dwarf extended, "Logan, good to see you. What brings you to my office?" Jeremy smiled.

Logan inclined his head toward Joe and squeezed, "Him, I think."

Jeremy let go of Logan's hand as he said, "Joe, this is my friend Logan."

Joe said, "My pleasure," as he took Logan's hand.

Logan squinted, "Do you work here?" Then he smiled.

Joe returned the smile, "No, we just meet here for breakfast and devotions."

Logan looked to the chair beside him, "May I?"

Joe answered before Jeremy could, "By all means, be our guest." Logan climbed up onto the chair.

Jeremy turned to Joe, "Tell him about your app."

Joe was startled, "What do you know about my app?"

Jeremy added, "You can trust him. I'll prove it. Logan, place what you have in your pocket on the table." Logan reached into his pocket, pulled out something, and laid it on the table. It was the largest emerald Joe had ever seen. Jeremy looked at Logan, who nodded. "Take it carefully in your hand."

It was so beautiful that Joe was almost afraid to comply, but slowly he did. Suddenly, in his mind's eye, before him stood the One Tree in all of its splendor, whispering softly his name. He was filled with an awe that was palpable and a fragrance that was intoxicating. It stopped his breath, but he wanted more. He slowly exhaled and then deeply inhaled.

Logan slipped out of his chair, "Follow me and bring the stone." Joe looked at Jeremy, who nodded and got up out of his chair, still holding the stone. They went out the side door. Logan pointed to a small sparrow sitting on the curbstone of the parking lot. "Whisper his name."

Joe was startled again, *"How could he know?"* but whispered, "Hasoos."

The sparrow turned to look at him and replied, "Yes?"

Logan said, "Tell him, 'the storm is coming, warn the others.'"

Joe did.

The sparrow said, "Thank you," and took to the air.

Joe looked at Logan as Logan said, "It's the Awe Stone. With it you can understand the animals. Come on back inside, Jeremy will explain."

Joe could hardly walk, but he made it back to the table, stumbled into his seat, and looked bewildered at Jeremy.

"Sorry for that, but you needed to know that you can trust Logan."

The single word tumbled out of Joe's mouth, "Okay."

Jeremy continued, "In the Garden, the fruit of the One Tree, when eaten, gave everyone the ability to understand everyone else. The Awe Stone was transformed from one of the seeds of the Tree's fruit into the stone before you." Logan took the stone that Joe had set back on the table and replaced it into his pocket. "Now you can tell Logan about the app. Oh, and incidentally, Logan's stone is only one of many that are being recovered."

Joe looked at the table for a minute to regain his composure, then began, "The world seems to be in an ever deepening downward spiral. My friends and I wanted to develop a way to separate us from the system. So, we developed an app that turns a phone into an untraceable ghost. It falls off the net and its calls and queries can no longer be traced. We call the app 'Archer.'"

Through the entire recitation Logan's eyes were wide. He finally reacted, "Jeremy, this is just what we will need in the coming days." It was a statement, not a question.

Jeremy nodded, "Yes, I think this is an answer to our prayers."

Joe furrowed his brows, "You've been praying for a ghost app?"

Jeremy smiled, "Not in those terms, but as you said, 'something to separate us from the system.' It has been prophesied that there will come a time when you will be able to neither buy nor sell without the 'mark of the beast.' Your app may very well be a way to get around that prohibition, at least for a time."

Joe continued to question, "And who has been praying about all this?"

Jeremy looked at Logan and nodded, "Okay."

Logan began, "There is a small group of us who have already begun to pull ourselves out of today's society. I think it might be time for you to visit us."

Jeremy added, "Yes, Joe, I think it is time."

"Ah….sure," Joe acquiesced, "When?"

Logan chuckled under his breath, "Are you up for taking a walk with a dwarf, right now?"

Joe nearly laughed himself, "Why not?" He stuffed his copy of "The Gospel According to Nick - Devotional" into his shoulder bag as he stood up.

Logan slid off his chair again and offered Joe his hand, "Following a dwarf can be a challenge, but I do a pretty good impersonation of an eager little kid dragging a big person along." Joe did laugh this time as he took Logan's hand, then looked back at Jeremy who winked.

Chapter Thirty-Two
Trip to the Farm

Logan nearly skipped along. He was clearly enjoying this. He inquired, "You don't happen to have a bus pass, do you?"

"Funny that you should ask," Joe blurted out, "Last week I purchased one on sale and had no clue as to why. I guess, now, I know."

Still skipping and swinging Joe's arm, Logan laughed, "Good, we'll walk to the transit station and jump on the 'Mountain Local.'"

"We're going to the mountain?" It seemed a reasonable question.

"The farm is out that direction, beyond Eiger Junction," Logan responded.

On the bus ride, Logan shared much of his story, from being in the circus, to finding the stone, to coming to the farm. It was an intriguing story and Logan was quite a good story-teller. Joe had time to only share a portion of his own story before they reached their stop at Eiger Junction. They had only walked a short distance along the road after the bus had dropped them off when a well trodden trail took off from it and led into the forest.

Logan confided, "There is a road into the farm, but it comes from the other side. This is a short-cut that takes us there from a different direction."

The trail opened into a meadowed hill and as they crested that hill, the farm spread out before them. A bench sat there at the crest and Logan climbed up on it. The sun had just begun to slip behind a cloud. The farm looked like a picture straight out of a magazine, so beautiful and idyllic. While not large nor imposing, it still had the feeling of something solid and substantial. There was a two-story house, complete with white pillars that supported a balcony and a porch of hand crafted spindles and a railing that looked out upon a large grassy, well kept lawn. In the back lay a well manicured, established garden and fields of corn and wheat. On one side stood a barn and corral for animals and on the other a building that probably contained machinery. Nothing seemed out of place and the entire place exuded peace and serenity, a calm oasis amidst the storms of life. Just looking at it made you want to go down there and experience it in all of its fullness.

Joe sat beside Logan to drink in the spectacle that lay before them, while Logan began speaking to someone who seemed to sit there with them. "Thank you for what You have created and established here and especially for those whom Joe is about to meet. Let him experience the welcome that only You can provide." He paused, then turned to Joe, "Well, shall we go meet some new friends?" All Joe could do was nod, *"Yes."* Logan slipped off the bench. Joe stood and took Logan's hand again. It was like having a little brother. While barely containing the skipping in his step, Logan led them down the path to the farm.

A man of indeterminate age stepped out of the house to greet them as they approached the back porch, accompanied by a large golden lab. As the man called out a welcome to Logan, the lab bolted from the porch to practically bowl Logan over, his paws on his shoulders, and tongue all over his face. "Lady, good to see you too." She released him and sat at his feet, her tail wagging ferociously.

Logan gestured to Joe, "This is Joe." The dog actually raised a paw for Joe to shake.

Joe knelt on one knee and shook her paw, "Hello, Lady." She licked the back of his hand.

Logan gestured towards the man, "This is Juan Carlos, he runs everything here. Well, his wife Maria really does, but you'll meet her later."

Joe wiped the back of his hand, where the dog had licked it, on his jeans before he offered it to Juan Carlos with a, "Joe."

Juan Carlos took his hand and pulled Joe into an embrace that would have been awkward if it had not felt so much like being welcomed home and into a family after a long absence. Joe actually placed his head on Juan Carlos' shoulder as tears formed in his eyes, and Juan said the words, "Welcome home, Joe." Those words unhinged him and he began to weep. Juan Carlos just held him tightly until the sobs subsided. Joe finally lifted his head and stepped back out of Juan Carlos' embrace. He pulled a handkerchief out of his back pocket to wipe his eyes and blow his nose.

Juan Carlos assured him, "Joe, you need not be ashamed of your display of emotion. It's quite common to those who first experience this," and he gestured around himself. "My wife, with the aid of the Holy Spirit, has created something very special here. Come on in, you're just in time for lunch."

There were places set for them, Juan Carlos, Maria, and their three children. Joe noticed what looked like turkey club sandwiches, chips, and glasses of milk, as the kids stood for the blessing before they ate. Juan Carlos looked to Logan and nodded.

Logan began, "Sometimes we speak to You too quickly. I want to take a moment for each of us to recall all that you have done for us," and he waited. Juan Carlos actually knelt at the table, holding two of his kids' hands. The eldest knelt with him. Joe wasn't sure what he was supposed to do, but he waited and recalled much of what had transpired to bring him to this point in his life. Logan finally continued, "for all of that we are thankful, including this food, Amen." They all added their own, "Amen," and sat at the table. Maria winked at her husband who had to get up before he could sit down.

Juan Carlos introduce Joe to his wife, "This is my wife, Maria, the soul of all you see here, including the food." Joe nodded to her, "This is Joe, he's a wind whisperer."

"What?" Joe thought, *"How on earth could he know that?"*

As though Juan Carlos heard his thoughts he explained, "Jeremy told us when he said that you were coming. Did you think we always made extra sandwiches?" and he chuckled. "He also told us you had something important to tell us."

Joe took a slow, shuddering breath. "My friends and I have developed an app that renders a cell phone invisible and untraceable, including all of its transactions."

The adults clasped their hands together, looked up, and mouthed the words, "*Thank You.*"

"Jeremy said you have been praying for something like it."

Maria whispered, "We have. You have no idea how it will help us in the days ahead."

Joe whispered back, "Jeremy shared with me a little of what you see coming in the future. Hopefully it will help for a time."

She affirmed, "It most certainly will. Thank you."

They chatted about the farm, their hopes and dreams, and as they finished lunch, the kids gathered up their dishes and took them to the sink. Juan Carlos turned to Joe, "I have something that you need to see. Follow me," and he rose from the table.

Joe got up, as did Logan. They followed him out of the dining room and downstairs to the basement. They walked over to a wall covered with a floor-to-ceiling blanket.

Juan Carlos pulled it aside to reveal a large opening where someone had broken through the wall into what looked like a tunnel. "We were trying to enlarge the basement when a friend of mine found this." He pulled out a flashlight and shown it down the tunnel which was suddenly illuminated in a soft red glow. At the far end, where the tunnel appeared to turn a corner, a large ruby hung from the ceiling. It seemed to have captured the light from the flashlight and was now displaying it back. In its light they walked down the tunnel and turned the corner. Before them lay a larger cavern. In its middle, encrusted with the drippings of the cavern like a stalagmite, was what appeared to be a large rectangular box. Protruding along it were two poles that extended from each side. Suddenly Joe knew what it was and fell to his knees.

He slowly exclaimed, "It can't be, can it?"

Juan Carlos and Logan also knelt, "If it had a cherub extending up from each end we would be more sure, but…." And he left the sentence open. Still, the entire cavern positively reeked of holiness. Juan Carlos stammered, "If it is the Ark, we have no idea how it came to be here nor how long it has been here. It does render the farm even more special."

Joe took a shuddering breath and stood weakly, "Thank you for showing it to me. And I thought I had a secret," meaning the Archer app.

They turned to retrace their steps, left the tunnel, and replaced the blanket. They returned upstairs and Juan Carlos gave them a tour of the rest of the farm. Although over-shadowed by what lay hidden in the basement, the rest of the farm itself was a place of peace and beauty.

As Logan and Joe took their leave, Joe promised, "Next time I return, I will bring with me half a dozen burner phones complete with the Archer app."

Juan Carlos thanked him and assured them both that they were welcome to return at any time. They followed the pathway back up the hill and turned around at its crest for a final look at the farm. They found the entire family waving good-bye. What a blessing!

Chapter Thirty-Three
Preparations

Once at home, Joe collapsed on his couch. He was emotionally and spiritually exhausted. He just lay there thinking, *"What's next?"* There were so many things that were appealing about the farm that he wished he hadn't left. He didn't even know if that was a possibility, but he entertained it anyway. He had never felt so at home as he had felt there. It was uncanny. Then there was the Ark. He could hardly wait to tell Jeremy about the Ark.

Jeremy began, while they waited for their food, "So, you saw the farm?"

Joe sighed, "It was much more than just seeing it. I experienced it. I have never been anywhere else that felt so much like home."

A smile slowly graced Jeremy's face, "Ah, Maria. Yes, she is a wonder. It makes you doubt that angels are only male."

Joe was shocked, "What?"

Jeremy continued, "Think about it. There are no recorded incidents of angels appearing as women. They are called the sons of God, and they took for themselves the daughters of men to produce the giants."

Joe stammered, "But the paintings of little cherubs with golden ringlets?"

Jeremy humphed. "How many other things have they gotten wrong? I'm sorry, I digress. You were talking about the farm."

Joe blurted out, "Did you know the Ark was there?"

Jeremy seemed surprised. That was unusual. "You saw it?"

"It is encased in the rock residue of a cave, but it had the right shape and drove us all to our knees." Joe's words came out in a torrent.

Jeremy looked off over Joe's shoulder, "Hmmm, I wonder how it came to be at the farm?"

Joe blinked rapidly, "Does it matter?"

Jeremy looked back at Joe, "Probably not."

Joe almost pleaded, "Can I ask you a question?"

Jeremy chuckled, "Number one, could I stop you? Number two, have I ever said 'no' before? However, it might have been better phrased, 'Will you answer a question?'"

Joe still begged, "Well?"

And Jeremy still smiled, "You'll probably need to ask it first."

Joe sighed, "Can I go live at the farm?"

Jeremy thought a moment. "That would be up to Juan Carlos and Maria."

"Could you ask them for me?"

The response was a quick, "No, that you would need to do yourself."

Joe looked crestfallen, "But they're your friends."

Jeremy chuckled again, "And you're not?"

"Please?" Joe didn't usually plead, but this meant so much to him.

"Nope, and that is my final answer." Then he added, "but I think your chances are good. Remember, you do have the ghost phones."

"Can you give me their phone number?" Joe seemed a little more confident.

Jeremy smiled again, "What makes you think they have phones?"

Joe frowned, "They said they had talked to you."

"Ah, they probably said that I told them about you, but that doesn't preclude that we spoke."

Joe humphed, "What'd you do, send a…a carrier pigeon?"

Jeremy laughed outright, "Yup, you guessed it!"

Joe frowned again. He was going to end up creasing his brow, "You're kidding!"

Still chuckling under his breath, Jeremy explained, "Actually it's quite reliable, just not as fast."

"So, what do I do, just go back there without Logan?"

Jeremy countered, "Weren't you going to take them some burner phones?"

"Yes."

"You can ask them what they think of having you join them more permanently while you're there. They may say they have to pray about it first, but they are pretty discerning. They might be able to tell you right then."

It seemed like it might be a good idea. "Okay."

Jeremy opened his devotional, "Let's see, where were we? Ah, yes, Ahlam, the consort, is brought to Jesus, 'In the Law, Moses commands us to stone such a woman to death.' You are familiar with this story?"

Joe had opened his devotional, "Yes, I didn't know her name was Ahlam though."

Jeremy's smile was back. "Poetic license, but probably pretty accurate. My favorite speculation is, 'What did he write on the ground?'"

Joe looked up, "I've heard it said that he started listing the sins of those who stood there to condemn her."

"Hmmm," Jeremy mused before saying, "I like that too. Well, whatever it was, when coupled with what he said, it worked."

Joe asked, "Did they really expect him to condemn her?"

Jeremy's gaze turned stern, "They expected to trap him, and it was quite a good trap. They just really didn't know who they were dealing with."

Chapter Thirty-Four
The Farm Again

Joe stopped again at the crest of the hill overlooking the farm. Even without Logan it had a similar impact to the first time he saw it. It was breathtaking. He was almost afraid to go down the hill, like his presence might mar its beauty and purity.

The kids were out playing in the back yard. So he asked them if their parents were inside. The eldest responded, "Mom's inside, Dad's in the barn." Joe headed for the barn.

Juan Carlos saw him as he sat milking a cow, "Joe, how good to see you again. Can you stay for lunch?"

He felt such genuine love and acceptance, "Yes, that would be nice. I brought you the phones," and he pointed over his shoulder to his backpack.

"Wonderful," he responded, "although you may have to help us. We are not very cell phone savvy."

While he knew that they didn't have any phones, he was surprised that they seemed to have never used them. "You've never had one?"

"Nope," and he almost giggled like a child, "the last phone I used had a rotary dial and hung from a wall. It was private though. We were not on a party line."

That was hard for Joe to even imagine. It was like stepping into a foreign but wonderful subculture.

Juan got up off his stool, patted the cow on the rump and picked up his bucket of milk. "Shall we go have us some lunch?" He closed the stall gate on the way out. They sauntered back to the house.

Upon entering, Juan set the bucket down and began removing his boots. Joe pointed at his shoes. Juan responded, "Let me see the soles." Joe lifted one, then the other to him. "Nope, they look okay." He picked up the bucket and walked into the kitchen in his stocking feet.

"Joe," Maria nearly squealed, "are you having lunch with us?"

Joe looked a little sheepish, "I've been invited, but if it's…"

She interrupted, "No, that's wonderful. Just go wash up with Juan Carlos while I get another sandwich ready." He could hardly wait, her sandwiches were to die for!

Lunch was nearly consumed when Joe finally screwed up enough courage to ask, "Juan Carlos, would it be possible for me to live here?"

Both Juan Carlos and Maria looked at one another. Juan Carlos asked Joe, "Do you believe in synchronicity?"

Joe responded, "Isn't that when two things that were meant to be together come together?"

Juan smiled, "Close enough. Maria and I have talked about the possibility of you staying with us, even prayed about it. Let me ask you a rather personal question. What do you think you could contribute to our little corner of paradise?"

Joe should have been shocked, but was not. "Actually I have thought quite a lot about that. If I sold my house and furnishings and moved here, I would need a way to reinvest the money without the authorities knowing about it, to keep us below the radar. I was thinking maybe you could use some livestock, but then you would need a place for them. Maybe some of the funds could finance that too."

Maria laughed, "I think Joe has been reading my diary."

"No!" he said shocked, "I haven't. I didn't even know you had one."

"I know, silly," she still giggled, "it's just more of the synchronicity."

Joe gulped, "Oh."

Juan continued for Maria, "I'm thinking an eight-by-twelve shed added to the barn, a twenty-by-twenty outside pen, and six to ten sheep. What do you know about sheep?"

Joe smiled, "Nothing at the moment, but I'm pretty good at research."

"Good," Juan added, "timeframe?"

"I've already liquidated a lot of things to finance the Archer app," Joe threw in, "maybe a month, depending on the housing market."

"Sounds good," and Juan extended his hand.

Joe looked at his hand, "You're kidding. That's it?"

Juan looked at Maria, who nodded, "Good enough for us."

"Do I need to spit on my palm or anything?"

Juan laughed, "No, just a handshake will do."

They shook hands.

Maria walked around and kissed him on the cheek, "Welcome home, Joe."

Tears filled Joe's eyes.

Chapter Thirty-Five
More Synchronicity

Joe had a cash offer for the house within a week. He probably could have gotten more if he had waited longer, but it wasn't really about money. He actually did get more than it was listed for because the buyer wanted all the furniture, dishes, pots and pans, everything that he hadn't packed up to ship to Elaine. The buyer wanted to turn it right around and rent it as a fully furnished home. Joe was even able to sell his car for a good price too. He turned everything into cash that he stored in his backpack, along with a change of clothes and a pair of sneakers.

During their final breakfast at Chick-fil-A, Jeremy pointed to the two guys that always sat up near the cashiers. "Would you like to meet those two guys?"

Joe shrugged his shoulders, "Sure, I guess."

They both got up and walked to the table where the two guys sat. "Jonathan and Nick, I'd like to introduce you to my friend, Joe." Joe held out his hand first to Jonathan, who shook it, and then to Nick who did the same. Jeremy continued speaking to Nick, "We have sure enjoyed studying your book."

Joe's eyes got as big as saucers, "You're *that* Nick?"

Nick blushed and looked at the table, "Guilty as charged."

Joe would have wagged his tail if he had one. "Wow! I've never met a real author. If I go get my book will you sign it?"

Nick looked him in the eye, "I'd love to." Joe scrambled back to their table, grabbed his copy of "Nick's Gospel," went back, and handed it reverently to Nick with both hands. Nick had his pen out and began to sign.

Joe asked, "You guys both already know Jeremy?"

Nick nodded, while Jonathan said, "Yup, we've known each other for a very, very long time," and snickered.

Joe looked at Jeremy, who just winked. "Do you also know about the farm?"

Jonathan smiled sheepishly, "Yup."

"And what's in the basement?" Joe said before he realized that maybe it was a secret.

Jonathan frowned, "No, what's in the basement?"

Joe looked scared, like he had committed a fauxpas, "Ah… nothing, I was just testing you," and he looked up at the ceiling.

Jeremy saved him, "Joe is just on his way out there to join them. I guess they need a hired hand with absolutely no farming skills at all," and he laughed.

Joe came back quickly with, "Heh, I resemble that remark," and breathed a secret sigh of relief that the topic had been changed.

Nick looked at Jonathan, "I think we have another trip planned out there in about a week. We'll look you up while we're there."

Joe started to turn away, "Thanks, I'd like that, and thanks again for your gospel," as Nick handed it back to him. "We are really enjoying going through it together."

Nick responded with what should have been expected, "My pleasure."

Jeremy and Joe both shook their heads, turned together, and walked out of Chick-fil-A. Jeremy asked, "So, how did you get here?"

Joe pointed to the bus coming up the street, "The bus."

"Do you want a ride back to your place?" Jeremy asked.

"Sure, I'm at the Marada Inn on sixty-fourth." They walked to the back lot where Jeremy said that he usually parked. They stopped next to two, three-wheeled vehicles that were tear-shaped like a rocket with tandem cockpit-like seating.

Joe exclaimed, "Shut up! You're kidding me!"

Jeremy laughed, "Yup that's mine, and that's Jonathan's. Pretty cool, huh? It's electric and a lot of fun to drive. Maybe I'll let you drive it some time if you're extra specially good." He opened the front door, reached in, flipped a switch, and the front seat folded forward. "Climb in. It's easier than it looks."

It was easier than it looked. "Do I get a co-pilot's helmet?"

Jeremy smiled to himself, "No, but buckle up." Jeremy was right. It was fun to ride in this little three-wheeled rocket.

Chapter Thirty-Six
The Children's Home

Elaine's reintegration into normal life was slow and measured. Once she had established the routine of working at the hospital and earned the right to Friday and Saturday off, she worked Sundays for those who wanted it off. She then added into her life the Sabbath services at the local synagogue, called Temple Beth El, the house of God. She began taking Hebrew lessons from their Rabbi. Joe had birthed that desire in her and she longed to cultivate it. His legacy to her was not all bad, just some of it tarnished.

Rabbi Jakob was quite good: young, personable, and devout. Still she did not betray that she was a fledgling wind whisperer. That might come later, if time allowed or required it. For now she just learned and practiced the deeper words when they were given to her.

For her devotions that day, she had been reading in Second Kings Five the story of Naaman the Syrian general who was cured of his leprosy by Elisha. Elisha had asked him to do something silly and he was initially angry, but finally did it. He dipped himself in the dirty Jordan river seven times and when he came up out of the water the last time, his flesh was restored to like that of a little boy, "Nahar Basar". Those two words kept rattling around in her mind all day long and when she got to the hospital that evening she remembered she would be taking care of a man who had received third degree burns over sixty percent of his body. He was not expected to live, yet she carefully changed his dressing while murmuring those words under her breath, again, and again, and again. It was almost as though she was bathing him in prayer. When she came the next evening, while sitting in the between-shift report, she learned that he was awake, sitting up, and cheerful. The doctors were amazed. When they went to change his dressing they had found the burns gone and very little scarring remained. It was a miracle, and there was no other explanation. When Elaine went in to check on him, he whispered, "What does 'Nahar Basar' mean?"

Elaine was shocked. He had been unconscious when she had changed his bandages last night. "Why?" she asked.

He looked her straight in the eye and said, "I dreamed someone was saying those words over me again and again."

"That's funny..." and she told him the story of Namaan the Syrian general and that 'Nahar Basar' meant the flesh of a young boy in the story.

He reached over and grasped her hand, "I was a general in the Syrian army in the last war. And if you check my chart, you'll find my middle initial is 'N' for... you guessed it!" Tears filled both of their eyes.

Elaine asked, "Can I pray for you?"

Still holding her hand he responded, "Please."

It was shortly after she prayed for Namaan that she began volunteering her services as a nurse at Abigail's Children's Home on Fridays. It helped her get back on schedule for the weekend and got her back in touch with a part of herself that she had somehow lost along the way. You might think that she was now working six days a week and would be exhausted, but her Fridays at the children's home with the children were more rejuvenating than depleting.

It was there that she met Piper. Piper's story wasn't particularly unique: turned out to the streets by a single mom who couldn't take care of her, foraging in the garbage for enough food to get by, living in a few cardboard boxes. When she was found and brought to the home she had only one possession, besides the dirty clothes on her back. She possessed a small wooden flute. She also possessed a large yellow topaz, but no one could see it unless she let them. She kept it in her pocket and you couldn't even tell there was anything in there. When asked where she got the flute, she said that she found the flute in the garbage and had cleaned it up. No one knew how she got the topaz. As it happened, one time while playing the flute, the ground had opened up beneath her feet to reveal the gem. Was that even plausible? No one would probably believe her if she showed them the topaz, let alone if she told them how she found it.

Her shoes had been deplorable and her feet infected when she came to the home. It was her feet that introduced her to Elaine. During her treatment she never complained, but often played lilting little tunes on her flute for 'Miss Elaine', as she called her. Her infection was nearly cleared up when one Friday during her treatment and playing her flute one-handedly, she reached in her pocket, pulled out the stone, and showed Miss Elaine.

"Piper, that is beautiful. Where did you get it?" Miss Elaine exclaimed.

She smiled, she did that a lot, "I found it. Would you like to hold it?"

Elaine was a little hesitant, "May I?"

"Yes," and Piper held it out to her, prepared to drop it into the hand which Miss Elaine had stretched out, palm up. "You need to take a deep breath and hold your breath."

Although that seemed a strange request, Elaine took a deep breath and held it as Piper placed the stone in her hand.

Elaine was shocked to find herself under water, and yet it wasn't water. It was like she was submerged in a lake of liquid joy. She wasn't afraid, quite the contrary, as her head slowly emerged from a lake and she found herself looking at Piper, only Piper was no longer a young girl. She was a beautiful young woman.

Piper said, "You may breathe now." Elaine didn't gasp, she slowly took in a breath that was nearly intoxicating. The lake disappeared and she was seated once again across from the young girl Piper. "Pretty cool, huh?"

"Yes, pretty cool," and she handed the stone back to Piper. "Aren't you afraid someone here at the home might take it from you?"

She responded, "No, silly, they don't know I have it. They can't see it unless I let them." She put it back in her pocket and Elaine noticed that there was no bulge in her pocket to show that it was there. It had indeed become invisible.

"*Hmmm,*" she thought, "*interesting.*"

Piper became one of the children who had lunch with Miss Elaine on every Friday after that.

Chapter Thirty-Seven
Sheep & Elaine

Joe was amazed at how quickly the sheep shack was erected. His funds had purchased the materials and like everything else Juan could do, he was quite the carpenter. The sheep pen was more labor intensive, digging holes for the posts, setting them, and then adding the rest of the fencing. The gate took most of an entire day. It needed to be just right, and it was. Late on Thursday afternoon eight sheep had shown up to call the farm their home too.

At supper there was a new young man at the table. He introduced himself and asked if Joe was the ghost phone guy. He said he was and the young man handed Joe an envelope. It was from Jeremy. He opened it and read, "Call this number…." Joe did and waited as the phone rang.

"Hello?" Joe was stunned. It was Elaine, "Can I help you?" Joe hung up. There was another page of instructions for the following day. They began with, "Be back in your room tomorrow morning by ten."

The next morning, Joe finished his chores early, played with the sheep for a bit and was back in his room just before ten as the instructions said. He had read them all, but did so again, "Begin by texting Elaine's phone number at ten"

Elaine sat at her kitchen table with Piper. She had taken Thursday as PTO and Piper had slept over. They were having devotions when right at ten in the morning, Elaine got a text, "Answer the door." She looked at it. It had no phone number, but just then the doorbell rang. She got up and went to the door with Piper trailing behind her. She looked out the peephole at an old, but vigorous looking man. Another text, "You can trust him." She had been watching him. He wasn't the one doing the texting. She opened the door a crack.

Jeremy told her, "Pack your backpack with a change of clothes, some PJ's, grab a toothbrush, and get your coat. We have to leave."

Her phone pinged with another text. She looked down, "It's a matter of life or death." She looked back up.

"Have Piper do the same," he said.

"*What?*" she whispered in her head, "*How does he know that Piper is with me?*"

From behind her, Piper grabbed the door and opened it, "Hello, Mister." She was holding out the Joy Stone in front of her.

Jeremy smiled, "Hello, Piper. You need to put your PJ's and toothbrush in your overnight bag and grab your coat. You are coming with Miss Elaine and I on a little adventure."

Elaine still stood there in shock. "*He knows the kids call me 'Miss Elaine'?*"

Piper grabbed her by the shirt as she put the Joy Stone back in her pocket, "Come on, Miss Elaine."

Elaine nearly stumbled as she back-peddled towards her bedroom, grabbed her stuff, her toothbrush from the bathroom, and headed back to the door. Jeremy still waited on her porch, Piper having joined him. Elaine came out, locked the door, and then turned to face Jeremy who held Piper's left hand.

He extended his right hand in greeting, "Jeremy. Sorry for the drama, but times are turning critical." He walked toward the bus line, but crossed the street. "We are heading out of town, not into it."

The bus driver greeted him as he handed him his bus pass, "Jeremy, all three of you?"

"Yes, please, Al," Jeremy smiled.

Al continued, "Some of your friends rode out yesterday: Jonathan, Nick, a woman named Muriel, and a young blind girl named Anna."

Jeremy responded, "Interesting, must be a convention," and he laughed lightly.

They started toward the seats in the back as Al called over his shoulder, "Usual stop?"

Jeremy called back, "Yes, thanks." They all squeezed onto a bench. Piper looked out of the window, watching things pass by outside. Jeremy addressed Elaine, "I know you have a lot of questions. I will answer as many as I can. You are familiar with the Ark of the Covenant?" She nodded. "We have discovered it."

Shock graced her face, "You mean like Indiana Jones, you've discovered it?"

He chuckled, "Not exactly. You are a wind whisperer?"

She furrowed her brows. "*Where is he getting all this information?*"

"What is the word for Ark?" he inquired.

She thought a moment, "Aroon."

"Whisper it and its deeper meaning." She did. "What did you see?"

The vision puzzled her, "A large subterranean cavern with a rectangular box-shaped object in the middle of the floor. It had a long pole extending from each side, but was covered in the sediment from the cavern."

"And your feeling?" he queried.

"Awe, but there are no cherubim. There should be one at each end."

Jeremy smiled, "I hear that a lot. We are going to uncover it."

"You know where this cavern is?" Her own awe was building.

He sighed, "I do. There will be other surprises too, but they will remain surprises, which means I can't tell you a lot more, other than that we are going to a farm which may be the most wonderful place you have ever been." He laughed gently, "Without overselling it."

Chapter Thirty-Eight
First Surprise

Jeremy stepped off the bus first on purpose. Joe had come to meet Jeremy, but Elaine hadn't seen him. As she and Piper stepped off, Jeremy stepped aside and gestured to Joe, "I think you've met Joe?" It was like she had walked into a glass wall. Her hands went up to protect herself and she probably would have gotten back on the bus if it weren't already moving away.

Joe looked at Jeremy, "He didn't tell you I'd be here?"

She barely shook her head, but Piper spoke up, "He didn't do it," she stated matter-of-factly.

Elaine looked down at Piper, "What?"

She repeated, "He didn't do it," and pointed at Joe.

Almost in disgust, she asked, "Didn't do what?" There was a lot of emphasis on the last word.

"I don't know, that's all He said," she added, pointing upward.

"That's what *who* said?" There was sarcasm lacing her words.

Piper ignored her, brought the stone out of her pocket and held it towards Joe.

"Wow!" exclaimed Joe, "that is incredible. Can I touch it?"

Piper smiled, "You can hold it," and she held it out to him.

Joe took it and his knees almost buckled. He slowly looked around, turning in a circle, to come back to looking at Elaine. He actually blushed as he handed the stone back to Piper.

Piper still smiled, "Pretty cool, huh?"

Elaine stammered, "You didn't do it?" Now it registered.

Joe shook his head, "No, I didn't physically commit adultery with Elise, but I was guilty of what I would call emotional adultery, the giving of my affection, attention, and time to someone besides you. That and my neglect of us was as hurtful as any act of unfaithfulness could have ever been. Can you ever forgive me?" There were tears in his eyes.

She nodded, and countered, "Can you forgive me?"

He smiled, "I already have." He chuckled, "It was part of my therapy."

Now she was a little stunned, "You went to therapy?"

Joe chuckled, "Yeah, Jeremy knows a guy…." and left it there.

She still stammered, "What about us?"

Joe cocked his head a little to the right, "Friends would be nice. Do you remember 'Gilboah'?"

She blinked a couple of times to make sure this wasn't all a dream, "Yes."

Joe continued, "I think what was blocked will be unblocked."

She sighed, "And promise again that you'll take it slow?"

He cocked his head to the other side, "As long as my slowness doesn't become a comment concerning my intellect."

She smiled slightly, "No, never that."

Piper took Elaine's right hand and Joe's left hand and the three of them followed Jeremy until they came to the path. Then Piper let go of Joe's hand and he stepped in front of them, behind Jeremy. They all stopped at the crest of the meadowed hill to let Elaine and Piper take in the spectacle for a few minutes before they went down to experience all of it first hand.

As would have been expected, Elaine fell in love with Maria and Piper with the boys, who had moved into a single room so that Piper and Elaine would have one of their own.

The next morning they all assembled with Logan in the basement. Jonathan was indeed there with Nick, who had brought with him Muriel and Anna just as Al had said. After introductions all around, Anna took a large ruby out of her blouse. Joe recognized it as the one that had formerly hung in the tunnel that led to the cave. She called it the Way Stone. They were joined by two other adult men who introduced themselves as Aaron and Jose'. Jonathan moved the blanket aside, they all walked down the tunnel, turned the corner to enter the cavern, and assembled around the large rectangular box that was covered in cavern sediment. Anna's stone provided just the right amount of red illumination. Jonathan stood at one end of the rectangle, Jeremy at the other. Nick stood in the middle with Jose' and Aaron on the opposite side.

Aaron asked, "Is this the Ark of the Covenant?"

Joe countered with, "Then where are the two cherubim that stand at each end of the mercy seat?"

Anna stepped forward, the Way Stone glowing more brightly on her chest, "They are here in person."

Suddenly, Jonathan and Jeremy appeared in glowing bright robes. The rest of them fell to their knees in awe and reverence. Elaine, next to Joe, sought his hand, found it, and held it.

Jonathan and Jeremy spoke in chorus, "You have been called to restore the Ark to its glory." Just as suddenly, Jonathan and Jeremy were returned to their normal clothing and everyone else found that they could struggle to their feet.

Jose' turned to Aaron, "I thought I was only looking for some sanctuary, but I think we have discovered much more than that." At his mention of the word "Sanctuary" a warm breeze brushed all their cheeks as a caress and the word echoed longer in the cavern than it should have.

The End

of this part.

More about Jonathan, Nick, Muriel, and Anna is found in *School Daze*

The rest of the adventures of these
and the rest of the
stone bearers is found in
Amidst the Stones of Fire
and
Out of the Sanctuary

About the Author

Bill has always been a story teller. His wife says he still tends to share the truth creatively and with a flair for the dramatic. He grew up in south Seattle and has lived in Tacoma, Washington since 1972.

He worked nine years in hospitals, completing half his RN education (if you had a heart attack, he could half save you). Bill joined the Boeing Airplane Company in 1979. The last 15 years of his 32-year career he taught Employee and Leadership Development full time. Bill often developed and taught his own material and has written numerous short stories and dramas, culminating in his first published novel, an apocalyptic work titled *Amidst the Stones of Fire* in 2017. Its sequel, *Out of the Sanctuary*, was published the next year. Bill then embarked on some Biblical Adventures. The Chayeem Chronicles are *The Magi and a Lady* (a Christmas Fantasy), *Hane and the Centurion*(an Easter Fantasy) (the Gospel according to Bill?), and *Zach and a Guy Named Joe* (the life of Barnabas, the first third of the Book of Acts). Then there were his two Adventures of R'gal the Archangel, *The Sword of Shenah* and *The Prince and the Soldier*. This is the second of his contemporary Christian novels which began with *School Daze*.

Now retired, Bill spends his time teaching, mentoring, acting in community theater, writing, and enjoying his family. Bill and his wife of more than fifty-five years, Nancy, live in Tacoma, WA. They have been blessed with three children, seven grandchildren, and one great-granddaughter.

If you can't find Bill in his home office, with his next book strewn all over the floor, then he used to be across the street playing with the neighbor's dog, Stacy, but she has moved on to a 'better place'. Bill will see her soon, but hopefully not too soon as he has started Book Ten.

About the Author

www.ingramcontent.com/pod-product-compliance
Lightning Source LLC
Chambersburg PA
CBHW072228190626
46809CB00017B/1525

* 9 7 9 8 9 9 0 0 4 1 3 4 9 *